Pink Icing

and other stories

Also by Pamela Mordecai

poetry
The True Blue of Islands
Certifiable
De Man: a Performance Poem
Journey Poem

for children
The Costume Parade
Rohan Goes to Big School
Ezra's Goldfish and Other Storypoems
Don't Ever Wake a Snake
Storypoems: a First Collection

non-fiction
Culture & Customs of Jamaica (with Martin Mordecai)

anthologies
Calling Cards: New Poetry from Caribbean/Canadian Women
Her True-True Name (with Betty Wilson)
From Our Yard: Jamaican Poetry Since Independence
Jamaica Woman: an anthology of poetry (with Mervyn Morris)

Pink Icing

and other stories

Pamela Mordecai

INSOMNIAC PRESS

Library and Archives Canada Cataloguing in Publication

Mordecai, Pamela
      Pink icing and other stories / Pamela Mordecai.

ISBN 1-897178-32-8

     I. Title.

PS8576.O6287P55 2006   C813'.54   C2006-903482-6

The publisher gratefully acknowledges the support of the Canada Council, the Ontario Arts Council and the Department of Canadian Heritage through the Book Publishing Industry Development Program.

Printed and bound in Canada

Insomniac Press, 192 Spadina Avenue, Suite 403
Toronto, Ontario, Canada, M5T 2C2
www.insomniacpress.com

Acknowledgements

In 1992 my father died and I wrote "Limber Like Me", which is the story that got this book going. So many other people have contributed to its development that it wouldn't be possible to name them all. I must call some names, though. Nalo Hopkinson, Olive Senior and D.M. Thomas encouraged me when I set out, a couple small buns in the oven. Nalo and Olive stayed for the pregnancy. Dionne Brand offered tea and I added another baby. Mary Cresser and Mary Jo Morris checked the fetuses, mid term, and pronounced them sound. Larissa Lai, Hiromi (hugs) Goto, Jennifer Stevenson and the Rum Bar Man mopped my forehead and held my hands as I screamed with the contractions, false and true. Timothy Reiss was a great godfather from the start and his practical support never waned. The inimitable Thomas Glave stepped in to assist in the last stages of the pregnancy. My agent, Margaret Hart, found them a home. Thanks, Margaret. My editor, Gillian Rodgerson, swaddled the newborns and saved them from more than one infection. If they are healthy, it is much on her account. Rachel, David and Daniel are, as Sarah's offspring, like the stars. I hope they like their new brothers and sisters. The Toronto Arts Council and the Ontario Arts Council saved me from hunger as the babies incubated. We are in their debt.

Some of these stories have previously been published in the following journals and anthologies. "Limber Like Me" appeared (under the pseudonym "Claire Marie Hitchins" in *Prism International* (Summer 1998). It was one of five runners up in their annual short fiction competition. An earlier version of "Once on the Shores of the Stream, Senegambia" was published in the anthology *Whispers from the Cotton Tree Root: Caribbean Fabulist Fiction* edited by Nalo Hopkinson (Vermont: Invisible Cities Press) 2000 and was short listed for the James Tiptree Jr Award. "Pink Icing" appeared in *Mangrove* (University of Miami English Department) No. 13 (2004). "Blood" appeared in *Stories from Blue Latitudes: Caribbean Women Writers At Home and Abroad* edited by Elizabeth Nunez and Jennifer Sparrow (California: Seal Press) 2006.

Table of Contents

Chalk it up

Every door inside this house have a window over it. Is not the outside doors, you know. Is every single door inside.

In my Granny house, is a real window, a window with glass. It sit sideways and twist to open and you stick a little iron pin in a hole to make it stay. In our house, is just a space over the door with pieces of wood shaped like the sun—not the whole sun, just half, right at the bottom, with rays sticking out and space between so the air can visit from room to room.

I need the chair, Papa's chair, the heavy one make out of wood that stay still and don't ever rock. Can't lift it up, me one, but it can shove.

This room is for us. Us is girls, the whole four. We sleep two and two in two beds that nearly fill up the room. I sleep with Carol for Papa say it is a better use of the bed space. Carol is first and I come last and Petal and Pauline in the middle. Petal and Pauline and Carol are in school. They can read and write and do sums. I can read and write and do sums too, but I am not in school. Yet.

I hear Mama and Papa talk about it sometimes.

"She is old enough to be in school, Evan. She can read very well. She knows her tables, right up to five times."

"Nettie, let sleeping dogs lie."

"Is my pikni that you calling a sleeping dog?"

I don't stay to hear any more that time, but another time I hear Papa say, "Nettie, she is good company for you. That is why I am not hurrying to send her to school."

That time Mama don't say anything, only sigh.

I don't like when Mama sigh. Carol say that you lose blood when you sigh and Mama thin like a chew-down pencil already. I fret that she going to just drop, plap, one day, if she go on sighing out blood.

Papa go to work every day. He leave early with Carol and Petal and Pauline, everybody brown and spry, crisp like a just-bake Johnny Cake. Papa look good all the time, when he leave in the morning and when he come home to eat lunch and even when he reach back late in the evening, but when school done and they get home, those girls look like boiled dumpling, all gray and wet with sweat in frowsy, crumple-up clothes.

I am a big help to Mama. Clear away the dishes after we eat in the morning and wash them standing on the stool, careful so none don't drop and break. Petal break a dish one time and it sweet me when Mama tell her: "Your little sister Colleen could teach you a thing or two. She wash cups, saucers and plates and never break one."

Every time Mama tell me something nice, Petal wait till she is gone then stick out her tongue and waggle her bottom at me. But Pauline take my side and warn Petal.

"How much time I am to tell you she is only a child, Petal? If you keep on and keep on, I going to tell Papa."

That make Miss Petal behave herself.

When I washing up Mama is taking a little rest. Sometimes she take a little cry too. I know when she is crying because sometimes I hear sniffing like she have a cold and sometimes her eye is wet and red when she open the door of her room and say, "Come Colleen. Time to read today's Bible story."

Is not one or two time I hear Mama cry. One time, I was round by the maid's room, looking inside one of the kerosene tins that we put garbage in. It was empty, for the garbage man come and gone already for the day. The only thing in it is a tear-up photograph in the bottom. I see Mama's head in one tear off piece, and Auntie Alice's head in another piece, and I think I see a piece of Papa's head too. I take out the pieces and put them in my pocket so I can put them back together when I go inside.

Just when I am pulling my hand out of my pocket I look up and see Mama coming around the corner of the house. Her eyes is runny and her face all wet.

She sniff when she see me, and wipe her nose on her sleeve, and use all her strength to make a smile.

"What do you have there, my Colleen?"

"Nothing, Mama. Just a penny I have in my pocket."

Is a big lie, so I tell God sorry same time, but I sure is better Mama don't know I find the picture.

I must hurry and get the stool, for breakfast gone long time and Mama still don't call me. When we finish reading the Bible story, we do sums, then Mama will teach me some history, maybe about the Taino people who first was in this island or the slaves that run away into the hills and turn into maroons.

I know is a long time since breakfast because the dishes finish drain and dry all by themself. Maybe Mama is sad because of the picture. Maybe she sorry she throw it away and she don't have another one. I take my time and put it together and I see it is her wedding picture for she have on a long dress and a long veil and she is holding flowers, and Papa is in a suit and he have a flower on his shoulder and Auntie Alice is in a long dress too, and she is holding a basket of flowers. Uncle Max is shouldering a flower too. Everybody is smiling a big smile except Mama. Mama's smile is not so sure.

I listen at the door but I don't hear nothing. Mama not sleeping for she snore when she sleeping, even if is only a short-time sleep. But I don't hear no sound at all, no sigh, no little crying sounds, nor no kiss-teeth sounds, nor no nothing. I take time and rap. First I rap a small rap and stop to listen. Quiet as the grave. So I knock hard. Listen again. Still not even a whisper of a breeze.

I think maybe something bad happen to Mama. Maybe it is on account of the photo. Maybe it is Papa that tear it up and when she think of that, it weigh on her so heavy she can't get up. Miss Clooney is next door and I can call to Miss Clooney but Mama and Papa say Miss Clooney get fat off of listening to other people business and I don't think Papa want her to know about anything in this house. And I don't know how to find Papa. He work downtown in government but I don't know which part. And even if I could find him, I don't want to trouble Papa for Papa is a serious man. I hear him tell Mama so.

"Listen, Nettie. Listen carefully. You know I am a *serious* man, so mind how you upset me."

I lifting up the stool. I going to put it on top Papa's chair so I can reach high enough to see through the sun window over the door into the bedroom to find out if anything bad happen to Mama.

I step up onto the seat of the chair and hold onto the back to steady myself.

I stand up tall on my toe. Good. Steady. Steady, chair.

Next I take my time to step up on the stool, then make sure I stand firm on it, and I hold onto the rays of the sun and look down through the space to see Mama. I don't see her nowhere. She not in the bed. Not sitting in front the mirror at her dressing table. Not in her chair under the tall lamp that she read by.

Then I see some frizzy hair peeping up over the bottom of the bed. Mama! She must be sitting on the ground. I hold on tight to the rays and pull myself far up on my toes. It is Mama, yes, and she is sitting slap bam on her bottom, looking at some chalky kind of marks on the floor. Her hand is holding a white stone, a big white stone, like from the quarry at Wareika Hill. But I don't see no chalk, so I guess she is writing with the stone.

Little most I say something to her. But I know that if she lock the door it mean I am not to go in there and also I am not to see what she is doing in there. I stay still and keep quiet and look, though is very hard to stand hereso and I am getting pins and needles in my foot. Right at that time Mama start to move the stone over the floor, and I remember that I have a big box of chalk that will write plenty better.

"Mama! Mama, I have cha..."

Mama head jerk up, and she ask a squeaky question.

"Who is there?"

Her eye search for where the sound of my mouth is, till she find it behind the rays of the sun.

When Mama move so sudden, it frighten me, and I stumble and rock the stool and it slip off the chair and drop and I drop and follow it, and everything crash down onto the floor in one almighty confusion.

For a little time is like I don't know nothing. When I open my eyes, Mama bending over me, crying. I don't understand. Nothing don't break, and Papa won't vex if we make haste and put back the chair and the stool, so why Mama bawling like that?

"Colleen, Colleen. Wake up, baby, wake up."

I feel a big cocoa on one side of my head. It hurt. I don't want Mama to cry no louder, so I only make a little moan when she touch it.

Same time there is a big banging on the window.

"What happen in there? Everybody all right? Miss Nettie, everything all right?"

Mama make no answer, only feeling my bones all over, still crying loud-loud fit to wake the dead.

"Mama, Mama. Miss Clooney at the window."

Mama still make no reply. I hold on around her neck and pull myself up but one foot fold over at the ankle and hurt bad-bad, so I drop down back on it.

"Oh Mary, Mother of Jesus, child! Have you damaged your foot?"

Mama say this when I boof back down for it hurt so bad a big "Wai-oh!" jump out of my mouth before I can stop it.

I glad Papa is not here for he is a good Jehovah's Witness and he don't like Mama to make any prayers to Mary, Mother of Jesus.

Miss Clooney hammering and hammering, calling and calling, but Mama lip still clamp up tight and now I am crying too, never mind I try not to, for my twist foot that I drop on is burning hot as fire.

I hear two people talking at the window, which is covered with a curtain. I can sort of see two heads through the curls and twists of lace.

"Eleanor, something bad going on in there but my eye dark. Look if you can make out anything."

"Mine no better, Minna. Can't see a thing, but that racket inside there mean something is badly wrong. I better use my telephone to call my cousin at the station."

Only one person on the road with a police relative and is she, Miss Clooney. Only one person on the road with a telephone and is she same one again. Mark you, everybody know is her son Lionel pay for the telephone, arrange to send the money from foreign by Western Union every month. Carol say Lionel think Miss Clooney is minding his little daughter who have sick cells and take in bad sometimes and he want to make sure that if she take in, he will hear straight away.

"Lionel don't even know that Miss Clooney dispatch Lesline way to Manchester hills, say the cool weather is better for her and anyway she don't have no time to nurse any ailing baby. That little girl could be dead and buried long before Miss Clooney know, let alone poor Lionel."

By the time Miss Minna and Miss Eleanor moving off, Mama not hardly crying at all. I hoping now they hear the quiet they will know everything is fine again and they won't bother to call police. I don't like police, for police take people and put them in jail to rot forever. I know because when Petal vex with Carol, she tell her, "You think you safe because you big. Bet you I walk down to station, tell police you beat me up, make them put you in jail to rot forever."

My ankle is getting fatter and the pain is getting big and round like the ankle.

Mama is not bawling no more, only tears drying on her face. She take her time and ease me up so I sit with my back against the bed. She take the pillows off the bed and put them behind me, then she go to the kitchen and mix sugar and water and bring it in a cup.

"Take this and drink it, Colleen," she say. "It will settle your nerves."

She look down at my big purple balloon ankle.

"That ankle looking very bad. I going just next door to call your Pa to come and take you to the doctor, only leaving you for a little bit," she say, same time searching in her handbag. "I have to pay Miss Clooney for the phone call to your Pa. You will be all right?"

I nod yes. She put down the handbag on the bed and look at the money in her hand.

"Oh, dear. Not enough."

Then I hear her in the kitchen fighting with the hard-to-open grocery money tin.

In the exact minute that the tin cover come off there is a big man-voice at the door.

"Open up this door!"

Mama run back to my side.

"Police, here. Open up."

We hear a next voice now and another set of banging.

I wet my panty—just a little bit though. Mama don't move. Just standing still like Lot's wife in the Bible turned to a pillar of salt.

Police only have to lean on the door and it give way, krups.

"Officer Clooney from the Trench Pen Division."

We hear him before we see a uniform appear at the bedroom door.

"My sister, Miss Eleanor Clooney, call in a complaint about a disturbance on these premises."

The other policeman behind him look down on me from way up high. He ask Mama, "Is this your child?"

Mama head move up and down to say yes, but her mouth is wrung tight as a sheet after you twist out the washing water.

"Please, sir..." I say.

"Quiet. Let your mother give her response," he say.

"But is me climb up on the chair..." I say.

"Hold your tongue, girl!" he say, sharp like Papa's big carving knife.

So never mind I try to tell them what happen, nobody will listen. All they can talk about is cut and bruise on my hand and foot, cocoa on my head, and my swell-up ankle.

"Where is the child's father?" That is Officer Clooney.

When they find Papa and he come home, he is vexed fit to kill.

"Nettie, how you could see this child come to harm?" Papa curl his lip in a ugly way.

Mama make no reply.

"You know what this is now going to mean? You are forcing my hand. Again."

Mama sit in the rocking chair, pushing it back and forward back and forward with her toes while Papa pack a bag full of her clothes.

Maybe she is going to foreign, I think, to the place where Mr Lionel is, where there is money to send by Western Union and everybody have a telephone.

Maybe I am going with her. I watch to see if Papa is going to pack a bag for me.

Mama get up and go over to sit on the sofa.

"Come Colleen. Come and sit with me."

I go and sit with Mama.

"Remember Jane and Louisa?" Mama ask me.

I nod my head to say yes.

"I want us to sing it together. Will you sing it with me?"

I nod my head to say yes again, and we sing.

"Jane and Louisa will soon come home,
soon come home, soon come home.
Jane and Louisa will soon come home
into this beautiful garden."

"Get yourself together, Nettie. The ambulance is here."

Ambulance is a big white van with red writing. Two strapping somebody dress up in white come in through our gate. One is a woman and one is a man, but she is broad and strong just like him.

Papa pull Mama up from the sofa. The plastic covering crinkle and it hold on to her as she rise, like it don't want her to go. I am like the plastic for I want to hold on to Mama too. I want to tell Papa, 'No! No! No!'

But I don't say nothing.

It must be because of me. If I was better company for Mama she wouldn't have to go. If I didn't climb up on the chair and fall down, no ambulance would come to take her to jail. There is a big stone in my chest. It won't even let my eye cry.

"Don't worry, Colleen."

Mama say this and she bend down and kiss me. "It will be just like 'Jane and Louisa.' And now you can go to school with Carol and Pauline and Petal. Tell them for me that it will be like 'Jane and Louisa' and I will soon come home."

Is when I am watching Papa walk with Mama down to the gate that I remember the chalk. I run inside, find the box and race back fast-fast to give it to her.

"Is nice soft chalk, mama, and plenty colours. Red and yellow, blue and green, even silver and gold."

Mama pat my head.

"Thank you, my Colleen," she say. "I know you will do very good at school."

The Burning Tree and
the Balloon Man

Sake of his missing fingers, Pa first turn into a tallyman, counting the loads of cane that come to the sugar factory from the small farmers nearby, and from Wentley Park Estate itself. It is one of Wentley Park's barracks huts they live in. When a old machine cut off Pa's fingers, they look around for a next job to give Pa and they find the tallyman work. Pa let them know he can write with his sound left hand for he could always use the two and they give him this job that he is better than qualified for.

The tallyman work never last long though, for when they see what they have in Pa, they move him up again quick enough. Is liaison with the cane cutters and small farmers that Pa response for now. And that is plenty, plenty people. Nobody don't call him no liaison officer, for money would have to go along with any title like that, but Pa know that if they never have him listening to complaints, finding small-size trouble before it grow up and turn big, the whole of Wentley Park would not be the place it is now.

Gracie never forget what Pa answer when her turn come to ask about the fingers, for they are not entirely gone, little finger-ends remembering what were once there.

"Is not so bad, Gracie," Pa say, and he wiggle them and make her smile. "Make me think of my own life, how one day it will dwindle down like these two, then vanish once and for all, like this little one here. Is a good lesson."

After prayers the children go off into one room with Ma. Pa and Gramps take to their respective corners of the larger space, the 'big room' where they eat and do homework and pray at the mahogany dining table, their one good piece of furniture. The big room is the room where Ma keep her few treasured things: the family Bible; a good set of plates (not matching, but with no chips); a "Home Sweet Home" oil lamp; a statue of Jesus carved in tough lignum vitae wood; a transistor radio they listen to the news on every day and, on Sunday, religious programs. Also, sometimes in the week, Mr Parkins' talk show, on those few times when Ma or Pa or Gramps for some reason have a break from work during the day.

In this Wentley Park place Gracie come to know that she must reverence the Most High God; she learn that the wages of sin is death, that pride goeth before a fall, that the mills of God grind slowly but they grind exceeding fine, that God is not mocked, and that she must walk in the fear of the Lord for the fiery pit is the lot of those who disobey Him. They tell her too that that the Lord is her shepherd and that God love her and will send His angels to bear her up — but not with quite as much persuasion as they bring to the terrible sureness of the punishments meted out by the Almighty.

Not Gramps, though. It seem Gramps and God have conversations all the time. Gramps tell her of things that God tell to him, not just things that he read in the Bible. For certain in the matter of cultivation, God seem to give Gramps special permission to grow some plants that other people are forbidden to grow. God and Gramps, Gracie come to feel, are often scamps together, though if you are God then you couldn't be a scamp. But if you make the laws, it make sense that you could break them if you want. It sweet Gracie to think that God change His mind and break His own rules. And it don't at all surprise her that God should give leave to Gramps to do things that others not allowed to. Gramps is special, and God is smart so He would know.

There is no prospect of Gracie being led astray as she growing up for daily she learn the disastrous consequences of deserting the straight and narrow path. Lying beside the bigger ones (Pansy and she with heads to one end of the mattress, Stewie and Edgar with heads to the other, Ma with Conrad and Sam and Princess on the next mattress, for they are all still sleeping together in the one shrinking room), Gracie listen to a susu-ing waterfall of information which start tumbling out as soon as Ma is safely snoring: who (whether big-big woman or reckless young girl) thief whose man, who make who pregnant, who lucky to lose baby and who not so lucky; who gone to the other end of the island sake of the belly they carrying, and who nearly dead sake of them try to dash away the belly. Other sins too, but there is no thiefing of stray goat, no destruction of property, no maiming a intruder with machete sake of praedial larceny that can compete with the sins related to making-baby matters.

Truth to tell, the niggergram can always count on Pansy and the boys. Unlike Gracie, there is nowhere that them three don't think they have a God-given right to be: first bench in Zion Holiness Tabernacle, and quick to examine the temple pool if there is a baptism; behind the counter at Mr Wong's shop, so make the old man get well vex sometimes; right up under the window of headmistress office, where there is a standpipe. You can go there and drink water or pretend to drink it, while you gulp the words that sailing out upon the breeze, loud and clear. These are places where you can hear every little thing and some big ones too.

It is the said standpipe where Stewie overhear the headmistress explaining to Gracie's form teacher that "The child Grace is not really the Carpenters' blood-kin, you know. Is adopt they adopt her."

The day Gracie get that piece of information was a day that she never forget—not for that reason, though. For another reason, having to do with what Gramps call "eternal verities", so that what Stewie say end up being no big thing.

Gracie remember it all clear as day, bright as a bolt of lightning.

Behind the barracks hut is a small patch of land where Gramps plant some yam hills and dasheen; pak choy and cho-cho and callaloo; Scotch bonnet pepper; skellion, onion, thyme. Ma too have some flowering plants there that are easy to grow: cosmos and croton, puss-tail and monkey fiddle and jump-up-and-kiss-me. On Sunday, and sometimes in the week, she cut some of these flowers and put in a jam jar on the dining table.

Gramps love to tend this patch of yard, which he refer to as his ground, and Gracie is his willing helper from ever since. And Gracie know that Gramps leave the patch now and then to walk some distance into the forest that start at the boundary of the yard and stretch out to cover the low rise behind and then continue on up to the hills as they get fat and full. Is right there behind the row of barracks huts that the hills begin and spread and grow to form into Karstic Country that bump up and down for acres and acres in the middle of which is the flat place which is Wentley Park Plantation. And in this forest, Gracie know there is a small clearing where Gramps grow some medicine plants, or so he call them. These are the ones Gramps has permission from God to cultivate. Gracie know she can't go into the forest with Gramps when he going to tend that plot, so she always sit and read and patiently wait until Gramps find his way back.

Sometimes he don't come back with anything but his

machete and fork, but sometimes he have bits of the plant which he call herbs and those times he would always let her watch as he carefully 'infuse' them (so say Gramps) into a bottle of white rum, and leave them to soak.

This particular day is only Gracie and Gramps at home, for Gracie is breathing with great difficulty and Ma is afraid she is heading for bronchitis and so she is to stay at home and be quiet and not stray far from her bed. But late in the morning, a morning that seem long as any day and night, she is bored, for she read every piece of old newspaper she can find, so she sneak out and walk up and down the narrow rickety back porch about fifty times, and she read all the words she can cipher out in the crossword puzzle that Gramps make sure to do after he drink his cocoa-tea in the morning.

They get the paper a day old from Mr Wong, and return it to him next day, for Mr Wong use it to wrap up codfish and herring and pig's tail. Gracie learn by looking at the puzzle after Gramps finish and trying to remember any new words and meanings that she can make out.

So, bored and daydreaming, she climb off the back porch and walk over to the back fence, a line of monkey fiddle straggling their gristly green and white stems and pink-red tips across the dark reddish earth. As she standing near the back of their plot of ground, waiting for Gramps to come back, the sky get dark quick-quick, and thunder start to roll, and lightning flash, and then something like a little river of fire lick the small otahiti apple tree that serve to anchor one end of the clothes line and zzzzt! pitchaw! pow! Right there as Gracie staring the tree catch afire and start to blaze.

Gracie so frighten she pick up her foot and take off into the forest after Gramps, never mind she know she not supposed to follow him in there. She race down the little track not minding the prickly things that jook her feet nor the long branches that here and there box her in her face. And she so glad when she see Gramps, she running, running up to him, fast as she can go, but she so frighten she can't get any words out of her mouth to tell Gramps about the burning tree, so she only moving her jaw up and down, and hearing no sound, and half-turning and pointing back to the yard.

And then the strangest thing, for, as soon as he hear the sound of her steps, Gramps swing round and shout at her rough-rough, "No Grace. Not one step further. Go back into the yard. Into the house. GO! NOW!"

Gracie is wounded. Gramps has called her 'Grace'. Not 'Gracie' but 'Grace.' Gramps never call her that. Pa sometimes; Ma sometimes; but never, never Gramps. In her heart she is deeply grieved; in her legs she is paralysed, for she cannot now move. Instead, she stand up stock-still, stuck into the ground like a yam rooted into its hill.

And Gramps have to turn around and shout at her again, not once but twice, before her brain reconnect with her foot, and she spin and race back into the barracks yard quick as mongoose, making sure to run round to the front of the house and into the bedroom and hide her head under the sheet on the nearest mattress and start one big cow-bawling.

But she don't turn and run before she see what is keeping Gramps in the forest. It is a man lying on the ground and Grace know he is dead for she see dead people before. Never never one like this man though, for the skin on his face and his arms and his fingers done lift away from his body and puff up like a balloon.

Gracie eyes glue onto the man as she see the wind, rising now with the storm that is coming on, she see it blow a piece of macca against the man's face and she watch the thorns pierce his skin and the skin hiss like a burst balloon as it break. It is in that second that Gramps spin round and shout at Grace the last time, and in that second that she find her two feet and run like her life depend on it. It is in that second, too, that her voice return to her long enough for her to scream "Fire!" at Gramps, and point to the backyard.

When, whispering in the bed late that night, Stewie inform Gracie that "'Eadmistress say is adopt Ma and Pa adopt you," Gracie just give a long suck-teeth, "Steuups", and declare with conviction, "'Eadmistress too lie."

Truth to tell, Gracie not even thinking about that. Is just the quickest way to deal with Stewie and his minor matters. Her head is full of too much other things: of how Gramps put her on his knee and laugh a soft-soft half-of-a-laugh and tell her he never know she had a voice so big that she could bawl like a bull-cow; of how he praise her for coming to tell him about the fire in the otahiti apple tree, never mind the storm was coming up and she must have been fraid-fraid of the lightning and the thunder; of how Gramps explain that he sorry to shout at her but that he never want her to come near to the dead man.

Gracie don't let him get off so light.

"But Gramps, I see dead a'ready," she tell him firmly.

"Not like this dead, Gracie. Not like this dead. Don't that's true?"

Gracie nod, yes, but she is not yet satisfied.

"But how he come to be in your ground, Gramps?"

"I don't know, Gracie. Maybe he came to help himself to some of the medicine plants that I grow there. Maybe he was so sick that he didn't know where he was going."

"Well, that must be a bad sickness."

"Yes, Gracie, he die from a terrible sickness that eat your flesh away. I see it when I was in the War. That is a long time ago but they still don't have no cure for it, and they don't know how it spread. That's why I make sure that we all keep far-far till the ambulance come this evening and take the corpse away."

Nobody else see the dead man. Only she and Gramps, and Ma and Pa from a far distance, when they reach home from work, but only the shape of the body for Gramps cover it with a tarpaulin to shelter it from the rain that she could hear lashing down same time she is bawling into the mattress. When all the other children come from school, they stay inside till police come. Is police and the hospital people that take the body away.

So Gracie don't care when Stewie tell her that headmistress say she is not blood kin to the Carpenters, for she feel deep down in her belly that by the events of that very day she has been bound even more closely to Gramps, and that, never mind she not able to balance a basket on her head like Pansy, and she not using no cloth for her menses like her big sister, never mind that, she is grown up in those minutes, in the time from the lightning hit the tree till she fling herself down on the mattress and start to cry. The dark sky and the fiery branch and the balloon man in the forest are big as any Bible story.

Pink Icing

For Dionne

We take the bus to school most days, but on some afternoons we go home on foot to save the bus fare. I say "we" because it is me and my sister Jennifer who go to Sacred Heart Academy. She is older than me and neat and always presentable, and she has lots of friends. Sometimes we walk home at the same time but it is not together. She walks ahead with her laughing friends and turns back every now and then to shout at me, "Why don't you hurry up?"

Most times it is just me and my feet and my load, and the dangers and troubles of the road. In the end though I will have my reward, so never mind that it is not an easy journey, I set out.

After school I take up my school bag with my books and pens and pencils in it and head out through the school gate onto South Camp Road. I cross the street to the side with the broad sidewalk because the sidewalk on this side gets thinner and thinner and then disappears. I make sure to hop clean over the gutter, which always has dirty water in it. The primary school children race boats made out of exercise book paper in the gutter, but we go to the prep school so we never do that. But we watch them.

I turn up, going past Sabina Park, and push my feet one in front of the other, for I am tired, past the enormous signs painted on the high Sabina Park wall advertising Pepsodent Toothpaste and Captain Morgan Rum and Sunlight Soap. Sister Cordelia says each day's small journeys are steps in the long journey of life, so ordering my feet step-by-step, I begin this small journey. I go by two huge old houses surrounded by wide porches and frilled with fretwork. No one we know has ever gone into these houses, never mind that they belong to the Ghysaises whose children go to school with us.

I tramp on, up towards the corner where South Camp Road meets Deanery Road.

Getting over South Camp is always hard, involving a dangerous lunge across the road, but like the nuns say about hard things, we do them because we have to. It is Sister Cordelia who always warns us not to make "dangerous lunges" but she cannot ever have walked anywhere or she would know we are forever making dangerous lunges *because* we take their advice about doing hard things.

But there are lots of hard things we have to deal with that the nuns don't seem to know about. "It may not be easy but you must find time to iron your uniform each afternoon," they say. "It takes determination but you must check your homework thoroughly," they say. They do not see us hurrying away from the St Joseph School boys who bear down on us in gangs of four and five, calling us nasty names. They do not see us rescuing our school bags from the gutter when the boys bounce us and make our bags fall in.

After I cross South Camp, I make another break for it, crossing Deanery so as to be on the side with Up Park Camp. (I wonder where is Down Park Camp. If it has ever existed, I have never heard it spoken of.) Again I put my life in peril. I know about peril for Mama constantly speaks of it. Life is a journey full of peril. It is always waiting for you, but if you face it with firm resolve, you can overcome it. Sometimes I think that I am only eight years old and should not be facing peril, but most times I do not mind because of my prize at the end.

There is no concrete on the sidewalk here, only dry ground with every now and then a weed, sometimes one that flowers, like buttercups. I walk past the gate for Up Park Camp, then I take the left branch onto Vineyard Road. I know what a vineyard is for there are lots in the parables that Jesus told. I do not know what a deanery is. I must ask Papa. He knows about words and their Latin roots. He calls them stems sometimes. I do not let him know I notice that what he calls a root today turns into a stem tomorrow.

The road is sort of steep here and my arm starts to hurt. My bag is heavy for it is full of books. I take home all my books every day because I am always losing them or forgetting the ones I need for homework. Papa says it is best to take them all home for it is "insurance". I know someday insurance is going to break my arms.

Now I am passing three duppy cherry trees near another entrance to Up Park Camp. It is not an entrance, really, but a place where miscreants have broken through, so the barbwire is stretched and there is a large hole in the fence. Though I am not sure what a miscreant is, I know it is miscreants who have broken through, for Papa says so. This gate is named "Duppy Gate" after the three big duppy cherry trees. The tiny fruit bear plentiful in clusters covering the tree. They are dark green at first and bright orange when they ripen. They fall off the tree and cover the ground and squish as I walk on them.

On the other side of the road is a big upstairs house at the place where Deanery Road and Herald Street meet. I know that upstairs houses have a meaning and upstairs people are important. That is because they are classy and have clout and almost always have colour. I know that from Miranda. She says she is not going to marry no man black like her. Not a chance. She is going to marry a man with good colour to improve her children's own. And it is not just any old high colour man she is going to marry. Only one that will put her in a upstairs house so everyone will know that they are classy people who have clout.

On the side of the road I am now walking on, there are no houses, only three levels of barbwire fence marking off the big green fields of Up Park Camp. That is where Papa took us to a Military Tattoo. There was marching and music and horses in lines and men in uniforms with high hats and acrobatic tricks. That was just one time. Every day, though, you can see white men with caps riding on horses in this place, carrying long sticks that they use to hit a ball. I think it is a stupid game for big men. I think it serves them right when the sun makes them get red like beetroots.

Today I am gazing over the fields, not looking where I am going, so I stumble and buck my toe. My left foot slips out and scrunches down the back of my shoe. I stoop to pull it back on and notice that my shoes have a thick coat of fine dust marking the deep creases across the front. No sooner than I get new shoes, they get creases and holes in the soles. Mama says I have a talent for ruin. The creases and the scrunched backs make her angry. Most times she just sucks her teeth and turns away but once she shook me hard and said, "For God's sake child! Money doesn't grow on trees." I do not mean to make Mama angry or to destroy my shoes. Maybe the dangers and troubles of my life make my steps heavy and that mashes them up.

The road dips again where Elgin Road turns off, at the corner where the Austins live. Somebody threw a stone and hit Norbert Austin in one eye, so now he has one good eye and a glass eye you must try not to stare at. I am looking across to their verandah to see if Norbert is there. I hope he is not for he will call me over to chat and

I am always remembering not to stare, and therefore staring at the eye I am not to stare at.

I slow down and am stepping quietly past so nobody will notice me when something runs over my shoes, first one and then the other. I scream and drop my bag. A huge lizard runs off my right shoe and hops across the road like it is crazy. I know it is probably hopping so because the asphalt is hot, but the sight of the jumping lizard makes my blood run cold. Then I see another lizard chasing after the first one. I jump away from it and kick over my bag and my books spill out onto the road and a car is coming and I am standing on the sidewalk screaming and screaming.

The car swerves towards the bank and I think it is going to hit me. The wheels roll over some of my books and two big boys lean out the windows on my side and bang the sides of the doors and laugh. I am lucky. Though the bankside here is not paved either, the grass that is disobeying the fence and crossing over from Up Park Camp forms a soft covering so when I fall and hit my knees and side and elbow, it doesn't hurt so much. I lie on the ground for a little. My heart is thumping so hard I can hear it in my ears. I feel something wet and sticky running down my top lip. I think of my handker-chief but it is not in my shirt pocket, nor my skirt pock-et, and I know it is not in my bag. I wipe my nose with the backside of the hem of my skirt, so the damp won't show so much.

I tell myself it is no use crying anymore. This is a peril, and I must face it with firm resolve. I get up onto my knees, then on my feet, and I brush myself off. I hurry to scrape my books up off the road, slap them together to get the dust off, and then pack them back into my bag as neatly as I can. As I tell my feet to start again, I look across to the Austins' house hoping no one has seen all this. I don't see a single soul and I feel better.

Now I am going past the Blythe property, which is the size of a small farm. The Blythes have plenty land and plenty more money, but most of all they have Tim Blythe, who we pass early in the morning on our way to Mass, herding cows on the road. He is a big white man and he looks fierce. He is the only white man, big or small, in all of Kingston, Jamaica, who at any time of the day or night is herding any animal kind. White people own animals, ride animals, shoo away animals, but they do not herd animals. But here is Tim Blythe any morning of the week, wearing high boots, carrying a whip and walking with his cows. We have never seen him use the whip.

We know why Tim Blythe herds cows. We tell each other the reason when, hurrying to Mass, for we are ever late, we whisper behind our hands as we cross quick-quick to the other side of the road. He is shell-shocked from the War. We do not have the slightest idea as to what shells might have shocked him (shells such as we know contain snails and sea animals) or what war this happened in. But since big people say this, their voices low, we say it too.

So here I am plodding against the long wall of the Blythe wilderness like the pilgrim in the progress. On the other side of this road are houses: the Singhs and the McCormacks, and the Champagnies who are old friends of our family and whose eldest daughter is named Jennifer, like my big sister. There is the United Co-Operative Store on that side too. Papa says it is not very successful, that it has never made a go of supplying vegetables and groceries to our small Vineyard Pen community. I laugh and think that it has made a went.

The sidewalk is narrow here and I am careful as I turn the corner. Now far-far in from the road, sitting in a large untidy space that cannot be called a garden, is the Blythe house. This is not just a big upstairs house. It is a white cut-stone house. It has a pair of twisting iron-railed stairs that meet in front to form a high-up entranceway, and a high shingle roof, and I can see it is a house much better than other houses. As usual, I do not see anybody inside or outside, not even Tim Blythe. We pass him on the road with the cows, and we know it is his house, but we have never ever seen anyone here, no one—not even him.

Now that I have turned the corner, I look back to see the "eyesore". It is on the other side of the road, one house away from the corner. (On the corner is Miss White; MISS White, with five children.) Beside Miss White is a large new home that burnt to the ground two months ago.

"Is not duppy burn it down," big people say with meaningful looks on their faces. "Somebody who feel they should get some, don't get none."

Also they say, "Dead-left, you know. It happen all the time."

Jennifer and me understand that if a duppy didn't burn the house down, then some living person did, but "dead-left" is a mystery. Still, we know how to deal with mysteries: we play the waiting game. We know that if we wait and listen, most mysteries in time make themselves plain.

I feel for my bus fare in my pocket, for I am always dropping things. After I know it is there, I change my bag from one hand to the other. I do this as soon as whichever hand gets sweaty and tired. A hand lasts five minutes or so.

On the other side of the road—I am walking a little more slowly now—are the Sabgas. They are from Lebanon. They are very fair but we know the white they are is not the white of Tim Blythe. On my side is another old house. It is a big upstairs house and the grounds are large, but it is not a house like the Blythes' house. In it live Mrs Farrell and her three sons, Joseph, Edward and Mortimer. Joseph has no arms and a very big head and he has to stay in bed all the time. Sometimes we see him at the window and he waves by bouncing up and down and we wave back to him.

Edward and Mortimer are well and handsome but

Mortimer is cold and smileless, and handsome is all it is with Edward. Mrs Farrell does not have a husband or money, but the house is big and they are white. They are Catholic and come to Mass at All Souls church, which is just up the road. We know the Farrells and they know us but we do not speak. We smile thin smiles and nod but we don't speak.

All Souls is next. You cannot see it from the road. It is a small church at the end of a long driveway. Since I know it is there, I make the sign of the cross as I go past. In addition to Mass and confession and benediction, we go to novenas for St Theresa and St Francis Xavier at All Souls. We hope to see Lucky Chang when we go to church. He is an altar boy and dark and handsome. He is friendly. Also, he does not make us nervous by gandering at us lustfully. I do not know what this means, but I like how it sounds and Jennifer says it, so I say it too.

I am walking faster, over the bridge that was built in 1938, nine years before I was born. I know because on it there is a smooth little square of cement that looks like marble and says so. Now I start to run fast-fast down the sharp incline, for I am anxious to reach. Also, as I run, I get a nice feeling in my tummy. Quickly I round the small circular entryway into Thrifty Store. Then I stop, and compose myself, and step inside.

I am here to get my slice of cake with pink icing. It costs a penny-hapenny—my bus fare. I do not like the cake much for it is sort of heavy, like toto, instead of light and spongey like Grandma Amy's. But that doesn't matter because on top is the pink icing that I have walked all this way for. I take out my penny-hapenny, and pass it across to the Chinese lady behind the counter. I take the slice of cake from her with great care, step outside the store, and begin by carefully peeling off the bit of wax paper at the bottom so none of the cake goes with it. Then I nibble quickly through the yellow part. Now in my hand is a bare, naked square of pink icing.

I take the first bite.

Hartstone High

Gyal, you owe me likl money
And you no have enough fe gi me
Come gyal beg you turn you kushu gi me
Make me rub out me money.

From "Penny Reel"— Jamaican Mento song

"Chiney-royal girl look like she can't mash ants!" declared Almina on the day that Shirley Lyn arrived at Hartstone High School.

Shirley Lyn had long black hair, which she wore in plaits that fell all the way to her waist, and fingernails that were pink and delicate with half moons that peeped out at the bottom and careful little pointy peaks at the top. Shirley Lyn's nails never got dirty and she didn't get ink from her fountain pen on her fingers. That was an achievement since not one other person in first form went through a day without getting ink on some part of their body or their clothes or their books.

Ink could do terrible damage, as, for example, on the Friday when Almina hit over her Quink ink bottle and the ink ran right through the crack in her desk where the lid was attached, right through the thin canvas of her school bag, through the brown paper of her lunch bag into the cheese and tomato sandwiches that she had brought for lunch. The accident was that much worse because Almina's lunch bag contained lunch for her two brothers over in the infant school as well.

Didn't the teacher come to the assistance of Almina and her hungry brothers? Well, no, she didn't, because she never ever knew a thing about it. As far as we knew.

The day Almina turned the ink over into her sandwiches was the first Friday in the Easter term. That day, Miss Latty did something she had never done before. At exactly quarter to twelve by the big clock on the wall of the classroom, she told the children that she had an important matter to attend to and wouldn't be back till after lunch. She assigned them exercises from their Raydon Rickards English books, asked Melanie Freckleton to lead the class in saying the grace-before-meals, and then excused herself and hurried from the room.

Shirley Lyn had joined Hartstone High School on Monday of that week. It was unusual for a new student to join the school at any time other than at the beginning of the school year, especially since Hartstone High was a pretty small school in a pretty small district and so, long before the school year began, everyone knew who would be moving up into new classes, who would be moving out of the district to go to the big city or fly away to foreign, and who would be moving into the district to join family already there or to take up a job that had been given up by a moving-out person.

So it was well established ahead of time what people would be going into which classes at the beginning of each school year. When Miss Latty explained that Shirley Lyn had only just come to be with family in the district and that was why she was joining the class at the start of the Easter Term instead of at the beginning of the year, sixteen girls were all ears. How had they not known about her arrival?

Miss Latty was not forthcoming with any more information, however. Nothing about where Shirley Lyn lived nor who her relations were. That was all she said, adding that she hoped they would all make every effort to make Shirley Lyn feel at ease. In fact, would everyone welcome her, please, with a round of applause?

During Miss Latty's announcement and the round of applause, Shirley Lyn stood staring at the floor. Her face coloured slightly but she said nothing. When silence found its way back into the room, she subsided into her chair and Miss Latty had to remind her, "Shirley, what do you have to say to the first form students who have just welcomed you so graciously?"

At that, Shirley Lyn stood again, head still lowered, swiveled her pinky-brown neck from left to right like a flustered chicken, muttered a soft "Thank you" and resumed her seat.

By Friday, the day when Almina spilled the ink and Miss Latty went off leaving them in the care of Raydon Rickards, the students of first form had discovered some of the story of Shirley Lyn's arrival at Hartstone. It appeared that she had not come from very far afield. There were Lyns in both Cavaliers, nearby, and Stokes Town, a bit further away. The Lyns in Cavaliers were plain Chinese, brown from the sun but with hair silky and long and straight and black as tar. The ones in Stokes Town were a large family of mixed up people, however, some who were almost black, some frizzy-headed ones who looked "like Jew people", and some who were "pretty and light brown with nice tall curly hair". The bloodline was predominantly Chinese in every case—they were the 'royal'—but there was plenty other blood mixed up in there.

All things considered, however, it seemed logical to conclude from the evidence on her head that Shirley was connected to the pure breed Lyns from Cavaliers.

They had also found out that Shirley Lyn had not succeeded in the General Entrance Examination that would have enabled her to get a free place to Carlton High School in Cavaliers, or St Anne's Academy in Stokes Town, or indeed at Hartsone High School itself.

That discovery gave rise to some speculation.

"It's true that they usually bright," Cinderella Latchman had volunteered, "but I hear my Auntie Fidelia saying that the dumbest girl she ever know was a

Chinese girl that went to school with her and that never even finish third class!"

Everybody stared at Cinderella, unbelieving. All Chinese persons in living memory in Hartstone had been exceedingly bright. In fact, it was generally accepted that all Chinese persons everywhere in the world were bright. It just was so. Consequently, if Shirley Lyn were Chinese but not smart, it would be truly odd.

Students could get into high school in two ways: through the island-wide General Entrance Examination, and as a special case student. Pretty much anyone who attended Hartstone had passed General Entrance—just as well, for Hartstone people were folk of modest means and simply couldn't afford to pay the full fees that special case students had to pay. Besides that, special cases could not be made for more than one or two people, it being only right that high school places be reserved for those who had won them fair and square.

Mr Fender, the principal, who was a man of great probity (he said so all the time), maintained this view, a position from which he insisted he was not to be swayed. The last Hartstone special case had been the grandchild of the Chairman of the Board, and she had graduated three years before. Mr Fender had yielded in that case, the Chairman clearly having brought heavier weight to bear than Mr Fender could sustain. But there had been no special case admissions since that one, all those many years ago.

So Shirley Lyn could get a place, if Mr Fender could be persuaded, and if she could pay the fees.

"She is well lucky," Viona Hamilton observed with a snort, having sat the General Entrance Examination twice to secure her place at Hartstone. "Her relatives must be holding a secret for Mr Fender."

Thus, for five days, from Monday to Friday, first form was happily a-buzz with the lore of Shirley Lyn's supposed family background and her academic abilities, or lack thereof. No one had figured out how Shirley Lyn's people could afford to pay the whole heap of school fees money, or, indeed, who Shirley Lyn's people were. But Mr Fender, everyone knew, was going to get every scrap that he was owed, down to the last penny. He was that kind of man.

So the money was coming from somewhere, even as the relatives must *be* somewhere.

Then Friday came, Miss Latty left class before lunchtime, Almina's Quink bottle flipped, and the life skills of sixteen first formers were taxed as they had not been before.

Shirley Lyn was in the seat next to Almina, and when the ink turned over, she wasted no time. Luckily, Almina had been holding her textbook in her hands, so it sustained no damage. While everyone else sighed and rolled their eyes and placed their arms akimbo at the extent of the confusion, Shirley quickly found her way to the front of the classroom and collected the chalkboard eraser and the metal wastepaper bin beside Miss Latty's desk. She also took up the jam jar in which were the hibiscus flowers that Miss Latty arranged every morning, having carefully transferred the flowers into Miss Latty's water glass.

Flitting back like a light brown ghost, she melted through the crowd of squawking girls to take command at Almina's desk, implements in hand.

Quick as Nurse with an injection needle, Shirley Lyn opened Almina's desk, dragged the ink-sodden school bag from it with exercise books and lunch inside, and slid it into the wastepaper bin. Then she mopped up what was left of the ink on the desktop with the blackboard eraser. Most of it had by then leaked through into the desk and some had started dripping onto the floor.

"Any chamois duster? Any old cloth anywhere?" This was as much an instruction as a question.

While people scurried round in search of absorbent materials, Shirley Lyn took the jam jar full of water and dashed most of its contents onto the desk and the rest onto the floor.

"What you do that for?" demanded Almina. "You want to make more mess?"

"Go on outside and throw all the things-that-spoil in the bag into the garbage bin, and then wash out your school bag in the bathroom," Shirley Lyn said quietly, ignoring Almina's question and indicating Miss Latty's wastepaper bin. "Run the water over the canvas bag in the sink till you don't see no more blue colour coming out."

Almina looked annoyed, but Melanie Freckleton, quick to see the virtue of Shirley Lyn's plan, shoved the wastepaper bin into her hand and hustled her off towards the door.

After that it went neat as a maypole dance. Cinderella found two chamois dusters in the cupboard where Miss Latty kept, in addition to the textbooks for rent, cartridge paper, chalk, glue, pencils, aspirin, a couple clean T-shirts and spare uniform skirts and, very important in the day-to-day affairs of the girls' lives, "ladies' supplies".

Sheila Murray produced a half roll of toilet paper from her desk. As usual, there seemed to be a lot of things in Sheila's desk but nobody got much of a look-see as it was always opened and slammed with great speed. Since blackboard eraser, chamois dusters and toilet paper proved not quite enough, one of the "ladies' supplies" was borrowed to finish off the job, which it did very well.

By lunchtime Almina's bag hung on a hook in the girls' bathroom, her desk was damp but not dripping, the floor was dry, the blackboard eraser was taking sun on the windowsill and Miss Latty's flowers had been restored to the jam jar. Things were almost as they had been, except for the fact that a clutch of admiring first formers now surrounded Shirley Lyn. She wasn't saying anything, but she was listening to the conversation, and smiling now and then as someone told her yet again how her quick-thinkingness had saved the day.

"I will bring steel wool tomorrow," she said. "When the desk is dry, Mina"—it was 'Mina' now—"can use it to sand out the stain. It will take a while, but most of it will come out. A little brown shoe polish will finish it up, good-good."

Almina swore she would do anything for Shirley Lyn, so great was her gratitude. There was some wonderment as to how Shirley Lyn knew so much about furniture restoration, but that passed. People knew things. Pansy Price could get a wart off with some strange concoction that she made from very dubious materials. Nobody knew what they were, but Melanie Freckleton's wart had fallen off after Pansy had put on the smelly ointment three times. To come back, it was true, but it *had* fallen off.

The lunch bell rang and Melanie led the form in a perfunctory grace. The first-formers were collecting lunch bags and pans and starting on their way outside, kindly offering Almina bits and pieces of lunch since hers had been consumed by Quink, when it struck Almina that her brothers would also have to be fed.

"Oh my Jesus! What I going to give them to eat?"

The further division and subdivision of their lunches and the preparation of a bag for Rupert and Appleton took a good ten minutes of the thirty-minute break, which was bad news. The gate between the preparatory school and the high school was open for ten minutes at the beginning of lunchtime, so that, under supervision of the teachers, big sisters could see and tend to younger brothers and sisters. After that it was closed for safety's sake.

Almina would have to hurry.

She hurried but she wasn't fast enough. The gate was closed when she got to it and her brothers were nowhere to be seen. She screwed up her face, not sure what to do. She knew that Rupert and Appleton would never tell the teacher that they were hungry: it had been dinned into them that theirs was a prideful family that did not ask for charity. But she also knew that they could not go for the afternoon without eating anything.

There was only one possibility. There was a track that ran the long way round, past the cottage behind the play-field which was Nurse's office on the three days a week when she came to school, and which served as the infir-mary on the rare occasions when anyone was ill. Having circled up over the slope where the sick-bay-cottage stood, the track then looped all the way around the infant school till it came to a stop at the front gates. If she hurried, she could get in through the front, find the boys and give them their lunch, and, with luck, get back to Hartstone High just before the bell.

She ran. By the time she was passing Nurse's cottage, beads of perspiration were trickling down her neck and into her collar. But she made it in time and deposited lunch with the boys who were so happy to see food that they didn't stop to find out any whys or wherefores. Then she started back, drawing deep breaths as she forced her scrambling legs forward. Exercise had never been, for Almina, a preferred activity.

On her way past, she thought she saw someone through the glass jalousies of the door of the infirmary, but she was preoccupied with the discomforts of sweat, fatigue and hunger and so she didn't look a second time. She just wanted to get through the last two class periods, go home, and forget the day had ever happened.

Miss Latty never found out a thing when she returned for the after-lunch sessions. Classes resumed with a lot of yawning, and school eventually let out into the joys of Friday afternoon when the bell rang. Perking up, Miss Latty led afternoon prayers, told the girls, "Have a good weekend," reminded them about home-work, and took her leave, and the harum-scarum drift of Friday afternoon going home began.

Almina had to go to get her school bag, which was still in the bathroom. Cinderella and some other beauties went with her to preen and generally prepare for any boys from St Anthony's High that they might encounter on the way home. Melanie had to go to the principal's office to hand in her prefect's report for the week. Viona and Pansy and Sheila Murray did their usual straggling.

When they finally gathered in a bunch in the school-yard, Shirley Lyn's new friends could find her nowhere. Then Viona Hamilton gave them the news that Shirley Lyn was still in the classroom, talking to Miss Latty.

"Bet you she currying favour, reporting on how she clear up Almina's mess."

"Cho, Viona," Sheila Murray drawled contempt at

this stupidity, "give the girl a break. You just jealous of her tall hair."

"I beg your pardon?" Viona tossed her sturdy plaits. "I don't envy anybody anything on their head. In it maybe, but not on it."

Sheila Murray ignored her response. "After Shirley never had to clear up the mess," she continued languidly. "The whole point of doing all that was so Miss Latty wouldn't know there was any mess. After she go to all that trouble, how it would make any sense for her to be telling Miss Latty about it now?"

For the next ten weeks of the Easter term Almina was careful with her Quink bottle, Shirley Lyn settled comfortably into Hartstone's first form, and Miss Latty left the classroom at a quarter to twelve every Friday afternoon and returned at the end of lunchtime for the last two classes of the day and of the week. On these afternoons Miss Latty seemed uneasy and more tired than usual, even sad.

But then it was Friday.

Now Sheila Murray, whose shoulders were stooped, whose eyelids drooped, and whose socks sprawled around her ankles, was not entirely of sound mind. Everybody knew this for a fact since it was amply demonstrated in several ways: she refused to let anyone see the jungle inside her desk, she frequently fell asleep in class, to the point of snoring, and—and this was especially odd because her usual demeanour was unenergetic, to say the least—she would, from time to time and for no apparent reason, decide on strange, even dangerous courses of action and, once having made up her mind, pursue them fervidly.

She had a serious attack of this recklessness one Friday afternoon two weeks before the end of term. The day had begun with a visit to St Martin's School for the Deaf in Cavaliers. All sixteen eleven year olds had turned out scrubbed and polished—well, almost all. Their pleats were sharp as a knife, their shoes burnished, their crochet belts bleached white as sea-salt. There were no inky fingers for sure, since they were going to have a practical lesson in sign language.

And extra time had been spent on hairdos. Viona Hamilton's thick head of hair wasn't in the usual short plaits but was rolled back instead into a lustrous French twist; Melanie Freckleton had an intricate pattern of cornrows; Pansy Price's head of short plaits had been combed out into a fullsome fro, and Shirley Lyn was wearing her hair loose. The loose Lyn hair proved a talking point. Tall it was, and black, but it had a pronounced curl. The Lyn locks were a confusing surprise. Perhaps, after all, Shirley Lyn belonged with the Stokes Town Lyns, those of mixed lineage, and not with the thoroughbreds from Cavaliers.

The sign language class had led to unprecedented discoveries.

The class began with everyone, Miss Latty included, coming up to the teacher's desk and placing their hands on it, palms down. It turned out that Viona Hamilton had a middle finger that was the same size as her index finger; that Pansy Price and Melanie Freckleton had heart-shaped birthmarks on their left hands that were in almost the same place; and that Sheila Murray had lovely purply-pink crescents that nobody had seen before because her fingers were usually such a inky mess. Miss Latty had slender fingers with half moon nails that plumped gracefully around the knuckles, and that were the dead stamp of Shirley Lyn's.

Unlike everyone else, Sheila Murray's hair was in its usual four uneven bunches, secured, as always, with of-all-colours-and-widths rubber bands. And the pleats in her skirt had that limp "it's the last day of the week" look about them. And there was a grungey ring around the collar of her white middy blouse.

Now, it is possible that on this day, the daze in which Sheila Murray usually proceeded lifted enough to make her realize that she was the only first former not looking her utmost best. And perhaps this insight was in some way responsible for what transpired at midday. Who can tell?

"Fed up!" Shiela Murray asserted as she banged the lid of her desk, stood up, charged out the door of the classroom and set off behind Miss Latty, mere minutes after the teacher had left at her now usual quarter to twelve. "Fed up of doing exercises from this Raydon Rickards book, full of squirrel and acorn. Going to get Miss Latty to give us something with lizard and coconut tree!"

Six girls sitting in the desks near the door crowded around it and stuck their necks out, watching Sheila Murray stride down the passage. Miss Latty had just turned the corner at the bottom and Sheila put on speed. As the huddle at the door watched, Sheila reached the end of the corridor and gestured with a flick of her left hand to show that she was going that way after Miss Latty. Past the principal's office she went, as she would subsequently recount, down the stairs to the bookstore, and then out through the main entrance, Miss Latty being now on her way up the track that led by the cottage—far ahead, but in plain view.

Sheila was still fuming when she mounted the stairs to the cottage. It incensed her that Miss Latty was sneaking off, leaving a dead Englishman to mind them with exercises about unfamiliar vegetation and strange animals. But as she looked into the cottage, it was Mr Fender that she saw reclining in the parlour, smoking a cigarette; Miss Latty was nowhere to be seen.

And then she heard Mr Fender ask, roughly, "Ready?"

And she heard Miss Latty reply, "Yes, you can come."

Mr Fender put out his cigarette, stood up, and pulled down the zip of his trousers as he walked into the next room.

Sheila Murray had not waited to see or hear anymore.

"Well," said Melanie Freckleton after a bit, "it make

plenty sense for Mr Fender to collect his on-the-side sex at school. Where else is he going to do it?"

Pansy Price, who hadn't started her period yet and lowered her eyes whenever Miss Latty produced ladies' supplies from the cupboard, burst out into a fit of giggling when Melanie said, "do it". Melanie gave a long kiss-teeth to express her disgust with this childishness, and continued her analysis.

"He is a married man with a wife and three children and a reputation to look after."

First Form listened keenly as she sliced up the whole thing like she was chopping grass for the rabbits that the Freckletons kept.

"If he was doing anything like that outside of school, everybody would know. So if he want extras, during school hours is the best time and school is the best place."

"Well, don't you think we should tell somebody?" Almina ventured.

"Who we going to tell? The principal?" Sheila Murray made a steuups to surpass Melanie's, pursing her lips and sucking a long stream of air through her clenched teeth. "If he want to go to Nurse's cottage, who is going to stop him? Whether on Friday afternoon or any time of the night or day! Don't he can just say that Miss Latty is helping him with something? And that they need to go up there for peace and quiet, so they can work without any disturbance?"

The bell rang, and Melanie swore them to secrecy during lunchtime. To speak of the matter outside would mean they might get Miss Latty in trouble. No one had even bothered to say it, so plainly was it understood. No harm was to come to Miss Latty, for the sin was Mr Fender's, not hers.

Shirley Lyn didn't want to go outside. She said her head was hurting her, so Melanie Freckleton gave her an aspirin and permission to stay in the classroom during the lunch break.

After school the conversation resumed under the big stinking toe tree just outside the school gate.

"Well," Cinderella Latchman said, "if he going to have sex with somebody in this school, I can't think of nobody better than Miss Latty."

Cinderella loved Miss Latty who had explained to her about periods the day she had started to menstruate and thought she was bleeding to death.

"Is true," piped up Pansy Price, "she is a nice woman, and curvaceous too. And she can make jokes. And she not mean. Maybe he is a very smart man to pick Miss Latty."

For Pansy Price this was a perceptive mouthful.

A good half-an-hour or so of discussion arrived at what had been said before: sex with Miss Latty was probably the best thing in Mr Fender's life and sex with Mr Fender made no sense whatsoever for Miss Latty.

Unfortunately, they could agree upon no course of remedial action.

"How your head feeling?" Sheila asked, turning to Shirley Lyn.

"It still don't feel so good," Shirley nodded thanks-for-asking at Sheila.

"So what you think of all of this?"

"I think it will fix itself," Shirley Lyn said, taking up her school bag. "I going home now. Going to lie down and see if the headache will go. I maybe see you all at the library tomorrow."

The next Monday morning when they had settled into their seats, Miss Latty began the announcements.

"I am very sorry to have to tell you that Shirley Lyn won't be coming back to school. She has had to move back to the city for..." She hesitated for just a moment, and then continued, "personal reasons. She asked me to say that she will miss you all very much."

They never saw or heard of Shirley Lyn again. Miss Latty never left the class to the mercy of Raydon Rickards on any Friday after that. There were no more reports of activity in Nurse's cottage on the days when Nurse didn't come to school. Mr Fender remained as headmaster at Hartstone High School and is still there, as far as anyone knows.

Alvin's Ilk

For O

Is a Saturday at the start of December. As Alvin is walking past Devil's Drop Down, a wicked dirt track skirting the edge of the mountainside about a mile from Chin's Self-Serve, he put his hand in his pocket to check for the money that Miss Mirrie give him to buy codfish, pig's tail, brown sugar, and a bottle of Pickapeppa Sauce.

Alvin never walk with money in his hand for he feel it restrict him. It make his hand sweat, whether paper money or "jingle money", Alvin's term for coins. Also, he can't deal with things that catch his fancy: can't pick up a flat stone to chip across Boatman's River, can't make discouraging gestures at stupid girls giggling and calling "Alvin! Alvin!" from behind their hands, can't climb up and shake down ripe mangoes from trees, or, if that can't work, stone them. And so on.

Alvin stop sharp when he don't feel the money. He sure he put it there and he sure it don't fall out for the pocket is deep and sound, being as Miss Mirrie always careful to examine his clothes before she wash them and if she spy any seam fraying or any little hole springing she mend them so fine not a soul can spot the stitches. This

Saturday, Alvin is most concerned not to do anything to upset Miss Mirrie, so he better not lose the money.

Miss Mirrie look after Alvin and see to his every need. The story as Alvin know it is that his mother and father die when he was small-small and after that his Grannie Elris look after him. The day he turn three years old, his Grannie get a stroke and die. He don't have no relation on his mother side nor his father side, so Miss Mirrie, Grannie Elris only sister and his only family in the world, take over minding Alvin.

As he standing there, fingers searching round in his pocket, he say out loud, quarrelsome-like: "See here, Lord, beg you don't give me no more tribulation, for I in enough trouble already."

Which is true, for he just get send home on suspension from school. That don't too bother Alvin but Miss Mirrie is heartbroken. When she open the letter from the school and read it, she say, "Dear Jesus! Alvin, is this true? Is you do these shameful things?" Alvin hang down his head and don't look at her and she put her head in her hands and start to bawl.

"Miss Mirrie, don't cry."

Alvin never see her cry before, so really don't know what to do.

"Please, Miss Mirrie. Don't cry. It going be all right, I promise."

But no matter how he try to talk to her she don't listen, just keep on crying and crying.

From Alvin small he feel something inside him jumping around so he can't stand steady, always have to upset things, disturb the quiet. He don't know where this nuisance come from that drive him to do these make-trouble things. He is just compelled to do them. Like you *must* climb a tree for a mango, once the mango is ripe in the tree. Like you bound to burst a empty juice box— "POW"—if it is right there in front of you to burst. Life is keeping on doing things because if you stop there is this strange feeling inside you, like something missing, or in the wrong place, or turning poopalicks over and over in your stomach.

Alvin don't see how he is responsible for this. Is just so he stay, and since he can't figure it out and don't know how to fix it, he is not too blaming himself.

Exactly as his fingers find the paper money (the pocket also contain string for a fishing line, a box of matches, and a couple of safety pins to make fish hooks) and he breathing a sigh of relief, he hear a voice call out, "Help! Help!"

He stop and listen hard but hear nothing more, so he collect a flat stone good for skipping on the river and he set off again for Chin's Self-Serve.

Central Village small and hide away in St Ann Hills but it still have a Chiney shop. The shop name 'Chin's Original Self-Serve' and Young Chin say it was a self-serve long before any other store in the island. First time only he was in the shop but when they close down Hong Kong,

Papa Chin come to help Young Chin. Alvin don't know how Young Chin come by his name for his face crinkle-up like wax paper that use over and over again: maybe he not old-old, but he far from young. Papa Chin now, *he* is well old, with his back curl over like a cashew nut.

No sooner than Alvin start off, he again hear the voice.

"Come the side," it say. "Come the side."

Alvin go to the edge of the cliff and look down but he see nothing unusual, just the steep drop down to the valley, with fat clumps of bamboo going all the way from the bottom of the slope to Boatman's River in the distance.

"Help! Help! Near the prickle tree!" This time the sounds not so strong. Alvin think he recognize Papa Chin's voice but he don't see how that could be at all. He look down the slope again, searching for anything that look like a "prickle tree" and he see some dildo cactus growing a ways down, wrapping the curve of the slope on the far side. Below the dildo he see a narrow ledge and there, crumple up and hanging on tight to a bush, is Papa Chin.

Alvin shout, "I see you, Papa Chin! I see you! I coming."

He about to start down the slope when it occur to him that, never mind that Papa Chin is small, he, Alvin, can't manage to bring him up by himself, so the thing to do is get help. However, he is also sure that is not a good idea to leave Papa Chin. He consider that maybe he could go down and light a signal fire on the ledge for somebody would be bound to notice; there is plenty brush and dry grass and he always walk with matches. But he quick to put that one side as foolishness for next thing he burn up Papa Chin and himself and the whole hillside as well. He decide that all he can do is pray that somebody come by soon who can go in the village and get help.

Alvin is a altar boy, so he know about the saints, and he know which one to talk to about this—St Jude, Helper in Desperate Cases. He begin, praying like Fr Michaels: "St Jude, please tweak the ear of God. Ask him to send..."

Right that very minute Alvin see Cheroot come flying round the corner heading up the hill on his bicycle. Alvin wave him down at the same time wondering if St Jude is really on the job, for Cheroot is not the most reliable person in the world. Some people say he is crazy because he drop on his head when he was small; some say is because he smoke weed; some say madness run in his family. Whatever the reason, Cheroot can't think of any one thing for too long.

However, today Cheroot is all that Alvin and Papa Chin have, for no one else is likely to come on this road, being is a track more than a road, favoured by Alvin because it is the shortest way to the Self-Serve and also because it pass by some choice mango trees.

"Hold up, Cheroot! Emergency!"

"See I-man here, Alvin. Where the 'mergency?"

Cheroot smile a full mouth of fine white teeth as he drag both feet on the ground and expertly halt his bicycle.

"Is Papa Chin, Cheroot—" Alvin tell himself to go slow and keep it simple. "He fall down the slope there."

Alvin point and Cheroot come to the edge of the slope and look down and say, "Oh Gawd!" when he see Papa Chin.

"You have to get help, Cheroot. Go to the Self-Serve and tell Young Chin what happen. Bring him back here quick as you can. I will stay with the old man."

Before Alvin can say another word, Cheroot is off down the hill, his huge afro of soft frizzy black hair bouncing round his head. Alvin sigh and he now ask St Thomas 'Quinas, who Fr Michaels say is a fellow with a big brain, to beg God keep things straight in Cheroot's mind.

Then he turn his attention to Papa Chin.

"I coming to you right now, Papa Chin," Alvin say as he walk around the hillside, scouting out the easiest way to get to the ledge. He eventually locate a stairway of stones, and pretty soon he is with Papa Chin.

The old man's legs stretch out but he squeezing himself up against the hillside, one hand grabbing the bush while the other hold onto the ground as if he is trying to push out the ledge to make more space. The ledge is not wide and not long either. Seem to Alvin he just have room to stand.

"Is okay, Papa Chin," Alvin say when he reach. "I send for help. They going to come and get us, soon-soon."

Papa Chin open his mouth but Alvin instruct him, "Don't say nothing, sir. Save your strength." Then he ask, "You break anything?"

Papa Chin shake his head. Alvin say, "That's good."

A little time pass and Alvin feel he should once more say something encouraging so he repeat, "They coming, Papa Chin. Not long now."

For a while they wait together in silence. As Alvin gaze across the valley past the shifting groves of bamboo and over Boatman's River to the cane fields on the far side, he wonder what on earth bring Papa Chin to that neck of the woods and what cause him to drop down the slope. He look back at the short figure on the ledge and see that the old man now have one hand resting over his heart. Lord oh! Suppose he have a heart attack and that is why he drop? Alvin panic. Papa Chin is not going to die from a break hand or break foot but a heart attack is another matter and Alvin is not at all happy at the thought of anybody dying beside him.

He study Papa Chin. His eyes close like he sleeping and he is not holding on so tight to the bush. Since he look okay for the minute, Alvin lean back, lower his eyelids against the sun and return to his own problems.

"What wrong, boy?"

Alvin eyes fly open when he hear the question. He surprise to see that the old man's eyes is still shut.

"Nothing don't wrong, sir," Alvin lie. "Try to rest."

"Okay." Papa Chin say nothing more.

Of course the old man is right, and things well wrong, all sake of the headmistress. Alvin have ten million reasons why he can't stand a bone in her body.

First thing is she talk like nobody else Alvin know. Not that big words upset Alvin: Mr Hector used to use them, Fr Michaels use them, and even Alvin himself try one from time to time. But headmistress use them like is things *she* have and *you* don't have, like words is to confuse you, not make you understand.

Next thing is she call everybody, "Boy" and "Girl" like she don't know a single person's name after four long years. But if you don't call her "Mrs daSilva-Meredith-Jones" every time you speak to her, you get a detention. It strike Alvin as mighty unfair.

But the biggest thing of all is her name: Mrs Albertina Rebecca Rose daSilva-Meredith-Jones. Alvin don't care about the plenty first names, but the three-part last name stick in his craw. After all, the Prime Minister have one last name. United States President have one last name. Queen of England have one last name. (Alvin think her first name is Queen.) Papa Chin come from China with two last name but when he turn a Jamaican he drop the second one so he is just Sam Chin. Alvin know that one-two people have two last name, but nobody in the whole world have three!

He resolve to make her know that she not so special.

He start small. One Monday morning, maybe ten or so minutes after the student body file quietly from assembly into class, there is a sudden chorus of "But Lord, what is this?" "Lord Jesus, preserve us!" leaping over the three-quarter walls separating the classes in the one long school building. Everybody concern to know what is the cause of the commotion. It turn out that when the teachers attempt to write on the blackboard, every piece of chalk in the school is soaked with something oily and can make no mark.

So pretty soon children of all sizes are trotting to the bursar's office to ask for new boxes of chalk. When they come back with the new boxes, and the classes are sighing, reaching for pens and opening books for the excitement is now over—more crosses! Every box of chalk is full of white powder.

"In my village in China—not Hong Kong, real China—is a hill just like this. Bamboo, all way down, just like this, and a river, like this but big. Wide."

The old man's eyes flicker open and take in Alvin then they close again.

"I was a tricky boy," he go on. "Head long. Make plenty trouble. My father beat me but no good. I tricky same way. Strong too. Lift any load. Run fast, climb good. Like you. "

Alvin not sure he hearing right. He see Papa Chin all the time at the Self-Serve and watch him as he tending tomatoes and beans and pak choy in his garden. But Papa Chin is not somebody Alvin like. He don't say much and always frowning as if he vex, and sometimes he wear funny clothes. Young Chin is okay. Alvin get a ride in his van now and then and he get jingle money for doing small jobs. Young Chin don't squint at Alvin, nor growl, nor show his teeth like a angry puss, all of which Papa Chin do often.

Suddenly Papa Chin suck in a breath and make a moan.

"Everything okay?" Alvin ask, fearful again of heart attack. "You having pain?"

Papa Chin press his lips together and shake his head.

"We tricky fellows," he say. "We tough, eh?"

Alvin wish Papa Chin wasn't saying "we" anything. He starting to feel guilty about some things that he do to the old man. Like Friday a week gone when he swear to Papa Chin that is he have change for Alvin, when in truth is him, Alvin, that still owing Papa Chin for the goods by the cash register. So he feeling bad as he listen to Papa Chin tell his story. And he confused as well because the old man's story is making him remember somebody, who as far as Alvin is concerned, Papa Chin don't resemble at all, at all.

Alvin going to Central Village All Age School from since he could remember. When Alvin was small, Mr Hector was headmaster and Alvin used to love school. Alvin could see Mr Hector clear-clear in his mind even though Mr Hector leave Central Village nearly four years now. Mr Hector was a peculiar man, jokey and serious at the same time. Even if he not smiling with his mouth, his eyes always smiling.

Not to say Mr Hector was a easy man. When he ready he clap you with the ruler. Sometimes he even beat you with the cane. But he never like to beat.

"This is going to hurt you, Alvin, but it going to hurt me more than it hurt you."

And you could tell that is true. He make *you* feel bad that he have to beat you.

Then Mr Hector wife take sick with some strange sickness that don't have no cure. And Mr Hector leave Central Village to go to King City for his wife sake. And Alvin can't forgive God for the next thing that happen: Mrs daSilva-Meredith-Jones come to take charge of Central Village All Age.

Alvin hate school from that day.

Alvin's love for Mr Hector feed the fire of his hate for the headmistress. When he realize that oil and powder, the things he use in his tricks with the chalk, are also things that are used for working obeah, Alvin is hugely pleased with himself. He counting on the fact that people will say that in all Mr Hector's time, no hint of devilry touch the school and now, look what happen?

Success make Alvin head light. He surprised that his plans work out so well. He decide to cool things down for a while, see if headmistress learn her lesson. All through the next week he looking for signs of repentance, but she is as full of herself as ever. So over the next weekend he is busy as sugar ants.

Monday morning come and as usual, all classes line up waiting for assembly to start.

Now every assembly go the same way: roll call, Scripture reading, prayers, then a hymn, then announcements. As teachers scrabble to open the roll call books, they find that every single one is pasted shut. Distress. Confusion. Amazement. However, by the time headmistress come out on the verandah to take assembly, she know the registers can't open, so she ready.

"Good morning, teachers and students. We will skip roll call today and go straight to the scripture reading."

As headmistress reaching for the Bible, Alvin see a look flash across her face and he follow her eye as it travel from registers in the teachers' hands, to the Bible, and then to the hymnbooks.

She suddenly make a show of looking at her watch.

"Insofar as I have just recalled that we must close early for staff meeting, we will cut this assembly even shorter. We will forego the Bible reading, the hymn, and announcements. We will pray briefly and thereafter you will repair to your classrooms."

Alvin nearly choke on 'forego', 'thereafter' and 'repair' but he give her marks for quick thinking.

A low mumbling disturb his thoughts. He realize Papa Chin speaking again, very soft so Alvin have to listen close. The old man is telling about his village and his life in China as a boy: about Chinese school, for boys only, where he learn writing, numbers and painting; about work in the fields after school, for boys and girls; about how one day warlords come to the village and he, Chin Fen Sam, is the first to see them coming because he skip school to steal oranges from the trees outside the village.

Alvin see it right before his eye as Papa Chin talk. See the young, strong boy, Sam, run to the village to raise the alarm. See the villagers flee and hide, the mothers' hands over the children's mouths to keep them from crying out. See the wicked warlords and their soldiers capture the crops, seize the valuables from each house, then burn everything to the ground, even the shrine to the Buddha.

Alvin listen in wonderment. He can't believe this old Papa Chin was once a strong young boy. He can't believe he could have a life like a war movie. And he can't believe that the scowling Papa Chin he know was once so bothersome that his father had to beat him.

In time, the old man is silent. When Alvin notice that his chest is slowly rising and falling and his hand has let go of the bush, he is truly relieved. Maybe telling the story ease Papa Chin's mind so he could drop asleep.

He now strain his ears to hear if anyone coming even despite Miss Mirrie's advice, "Watch a pot, it never boil."

And true to tell it seem like Alvin is listening and listening for a good enough time before Young Chin come in his van. Still, when the van reach, no sooner than Alvin hear brakes mashing than Young Chin appear at the edge of the ledge, squeezing his small feet into the bit of space that is left.

Alvin say soft to the old man, "See Papa Chin, them come." Then he say to young Chin, "I will go up now and give a hand up there."

He reach up to the road and see Cheroot with two of the mechanics from the We Repair Anything Garage.

"I too glad to see you, Cheroot," Alvin say. Cheroot smile from one ear to the next one.

The four of them pull his bike from out the van, then a big basket-looking thing. Alvin see that it is the wicker chair that hang from the ceiling of the Chin's front porch. The two mechanic fellows have some stout ropes that they fasten to the chair. They tie the other ends to a guango tree, then Alvin and Cheroot and the two of them stand, two in front and two behind, and use the ropes to let the chair down the hillside.

"I get it. I get it," Chin call out. Little later he shout again, "Pull!"

They ease the chair up with Papa Chin holding tight to the sides. The mechanic fellows lift Papa Chin and prop him up on pillows in the back of the van.

"Can't say enough thank you, Alvin, Cheroot," Young Chin say. "I going now. I see you later at the shop."

Alvin suddenly realize that like how he don't come back from the shop, Miss Mirrie must be worried.

"Please if you could send a message to Miss Mirrie to say what happen, Mr Chin?" he ask. "I was coming to buy things for her at the Self-Serve."

"I make sure she get the message, Alvin. You tell me

what things she want and I send them same time."

"Pound of codfish, pound of pig-tail, bag of brown sugar, one bottle Pickapeppa sauce." Alvin reel them off. "And see the money here, sir." Alvin dig into his pocket.

Young Chin say, "Don't bother with no money, Alvin. Give back to Miss Mirrie." Then he squeeze into the front of the van with the mechanics and drive off.

Alvin and Cheroot watch the van disappear, then they turn back up the road, Cheroot pushing his bike, Alvin walking side of him.

"Alvin, you know what happen at school yesterday..."

"What happen like what?" Alvin ask.

"You don't hear?" Cheroot sound pleased Alvin don't know, glad to be giving him important information. "Mrs Ballen find the criminal that make all the trouble."

"True?"

Alvin can't figure this one.

"True, yes. They send for police and they going try him at court house in St Ann's Bay and lock him in jail."

Alvin stop and face Cheroot. "So you know who the criminal is?"

Cheroot shake his head and look disappointed. "I think it must be somebody well smart."

He sound envious.

"So nobody know is who?"

"Some say is a big boy. Some say is a girl small so she can hide easy. Some say it must be a duppy for nobody never see him."

"Well," Alvin say, "I guess we will soon know."

By now they reach Miss Mirrie's house.

"Okay Alvin," Cheroot say. "See you Monday at school."

"Thanks for reaching the Self-Serve so quick, Cheroot. Is you make it all come out okay."

Alvin don't grudge Cheroot the praise. He tired to hear people laugh at Cheroot and call him stupid.

"Cho, that's okay man." Cheroot jump on the bike. "I gone now." And so saying he start to pump the bicycle up the hill.

When Alvin go inside, Miss Mirrie is waiting for him. He go in as always by the back door and he see her sitting down at the kitchen table knitting, with the things from Chin's Self-Serve in front of her.

"I see you reach."

"Yes'm."

She sign to Alvin to sit in the chair across from her. He sit. He look at his hands, on the ground, out the window, but he don't look at Miss Mirrie. At last Miss Mirrie stop and fold the bright blue sweater she is knitting for Alvin over the ball of wool.

"Alvin," she say. "You know my heart not good. Is kill you trying to kill me?"

Alvin shake his head vigorously to say no.

"I glad to hear for I don't know what to make of this. In two days, I hear the worst and the best of you. I hope the good things is right and the bad things is wrong. But you better give me a full report, for when I go to see the lady headmistress, I need to have things straight in my mind."

"Is true about Papa Chin, Miss Mirrie," Alvin raise his head and look at her for the first time. "And I don't know what the letter say, but I going tell you all about what happen at school. Everything."

"Go on."

"I fix up the chalk one day so it can't write. Is not plenty, just the little box they give each class to start the week. I use coconut oil and put on them. And then," he going slower now, and his voice get softer, "then I fix it so that all the chalk in the boxes what leave is mash up into powder."

"You need to speak up, Alvin. Nothing is wrong with my ears and I am having a hard time hearing what you saying."

Alvin feel Miss Mirrie's eyes making a hole through his forehead, looking into his mind, and he don't want her to find out about the thing moving about inside him that push him to make all this trouble.

"And another time I paste up the registers, and the Bible and the hymn books."

Miss Mirrie's eyebrows raise up and pleat her forehead.

"So how you one manage to do all of this damage?"

"How I fix the chalk and paste up the books, Miss Mirrie? Easy. You know Fr Michaels have a set of keys for the office and the hall and the shop and everything at the school?"

Miss Mirrie nod yes.

"I just borrow them when I go to altar boys' meeting. Put them back next morning when I go to serve at Mass."

"So you come and go in the school premises as you please?"

Alvin nod.

"How come nobody see you? And when you get the time to do all this?"

"I do it after altar boys' meeting. Nobody at school those times. And I work fast."

"Indeed."

Alvin not sure what Miss Mirrie mean by this.

"Miss Mirrie, Mistress daSilva-Meredith-Jones..." he begin by way of trying to explain himself, "she is not a nice woman..."

Miss Mirrie cut him off.

"I don't ask you for no account of the headmistress, Alvin. I can take that account myself. You best study your book now. I have plenty things to think about. And no altar boys' meeting tonight."

Alvin want very much for Miss Mirrie to understand how he feel: about school, about the three-name head-mistress, about the thing moving round inside him. But he don't understand these things too well himself. And there is one last thing he have to tell Miss Mirrie. He don't know why he hold it back, for it not worse than any of the other things. Maybe because that is the time when he discover the name for the thing so long moving around inside him, and because, like spite, it is from Mrs daSilva-Meredith-Jones that he discover it.

At the end of the second week, when headmistress show no sign of a change in her ways, Alvin decide to make another effort to cut her down to size. That weekend he do his best work. On Monday, everybody arrive at school to see yards and yards of toilet paper weaving through the leaves and branches of the big mango tree in the schoolyard and decorating all the aloe plants that line the driveway to the school gates. Enough toilet paper to supply the school for one whole month!

At assembly headmistress rave so much about the decorations that foam-banks of spit collect at her mouth-corner.

"I hope the perpetrator of these acts recognizes that this is an infraction of the laws of the land!" she say at the top of her voice.

Then she drop the bomb.

"I am going to keep the whole school standing outside in the sun till the vicious prankster identifies himself."

Break time come. Sun beating down but nobody own up. Mrs Three-Name come back out. She shoulder Mrs Ballen, the deputy head who been standing with the children all morning in the sun, out of the way, grab the lectern and glare at students who are wiping away sweat with their sleeves or flashing it off with their fingers. As Alvin see her face, he know she come to send them into class, and he know why: parents going be well vex if she keep them there the whole day. Still she have to let them off without looking bad.

"Since this criminal is determined to defy authority, I have decided to let the police handle matters." She talking quick and brisk. "They will find the culprit and incarcerate him in a jail cell where all persons of his ilk belong."

Alvin standing close to the back, watching Mrs daSilva Meredith-Jones' eyes get small-small, hearing her sound like she well pleased that police going haul somebody off to jail, listening as she say "all persons of his ilk". Alvin know he is the culprit, therefore he must be the one with the ilk.

How is it, he wonder, that all this time he never know that the thing moving around in his body is a ilk?

Nobody hear nothing further until Thursday morning assembly which is taken by Mrs Ballen. At announcement time, she bring the news that headmistress is gone to King City. Seem to Alvin that the air is fresher, the sun is brighter and the lessons is easier over the next two days. On Friday, he on his way out the school gate when a small boy stop him and say that Mrs Ballen want to see him.

"Alvin, I'm just going to ask you one question, and I'm counting on you to tell the truth." Mrs Ballen sit forward in her chair. "Are you responsible for all this trouble?"

Alvin eyes make four with hers and he nod.

"I am really very sorry to hear that but I'm glad you owned up. It counts in your favour."

Alvin look down, smiling on one side of his mouth.

The smile don't escape Mrs Ballen.

"I hope you realize this is a serious matter. I've talked with your class teacher. She says you are a good student. None of your teachers has any complaints about your behaviour. Nonetheless, you will have to be punished. I am obliged to suspend you for the rest of the term and ask your guardian to see me."

That upset Alvin.

"Please, Miss..."

"Please take this letter home to her, Alvin. Can I trust you to do that?"

"Yes ma'am."

"Very well. You may go now. I'll ask Cheroot to bring both the schoolwork and homework for you, so you don't fall behind."

Peenie wallies outside blinking their lights up and down in the crotons when Alvin realize that he don't start studying yet. He sigh and open his book, glad that at least Miss Mirrie is talking to him again.

Next day, Saturday, Alvin go with Miss Mirrie and a group from church on a pilgrimage to the national shrine, so they gone whole day. He get plenty praises for rescuing Papa Chin, but he know in time those same people will hear he is suspended from school.

On Monday morning Miss Mirrie tell Alvin to go up by the Self-Serve to see how Papa Chin is doing. When he see Miss Evangeline in the shop, he get concerned, for she help the Chins in the house but she don't hardly come down to the shop.

"Morning, Miss Vange. How Papa Chin?"

"Not too bad, Alvin. Not too bad."

"They know as yet what sick him, make him fall down?"

"Well, the old man can't remember nothing. Doctor examine him and say he must go to Long Shore Hospital for tests, so he going tomorrow. God bless that you find him and handle everything so good, Alvin. Miss Mirrie must be proud of you."

"Is not anything, ma'am, just what any right-thinking person would do."

"No denying that, but not everybody is right think-ing." She smile. It turn her cheeks into two sugar loaf hills and crinkle her eyes up till they disappear. "Young Mr Chin say if you come by to send you up to the house."

Alvin don't want to go but he know he can't refuse, so he say, "Okay ma'am" and turn to go outside to the road.

"Shorter if you come this way, son. Pass through Papa Chin courtyard."

Miss Evangeline direct Alvin to a corridor leading to the back of the shop. Alvin walk through the darkish hallway and come down the steps to find himself on a square of concrete paving that have pots of plants all around. He blink for the place shady and cool like riverside, never mind the sun well hot. Same time Young Chin come out on the back porch of the house on the other side of the space.

"Alvin, I got to go back to the shop now. You could stay with the old man till Miss Vange come up?"

Alvin feel sort of strange for he never go into the Chin house before, but he say "Yes sir." Young Chin call him up onto the porch, and then show him inside to a room where Papa Chin is lying on a bed with eyes closed.

"Miss Vange coming right over, Alvin," Young Chin say. "You would like something to drink? Maybe some butterfly biscuit?"

Alvin say "Yes, thanks," and Young Chin make a slight bow and vanish quiet like a mus-mus.

Alvin look at Papa Chin whose chest is slightly rising and falling, just like when he was sleeping on the ledge. The old man is wearing a white short-sleeved T-shirt with a V-neck that show a chest with a few gray hairs and skin that is dark. That make Alvin consider. He think is natural for the sun to make the old man's face and forearms dark, but he well surprised that his chest and upper arms are also brown.

Alvin lean forward to look at chest and arms, and just that minute the old man open his eyes and ask, "What you looking at, long-head boy?"

It take Alvin so much by surprise, he just blurt out, "At how come you dark all over, Papa Chin..."

Papa Chin don't answer straightaway.

"Plenty thing same. When you grow, you know."

He yawn and scratch his head but he don't take his eyes off Alvin. The slant at each eye corner is like a little grin.

"Me Hakka," he say in his same growling voice. "Hakka not rich. Workers. Don't live one place. Go all over south of China, go where work is. Hakka people dark. Strong. Work hard and live long."

It seem that in a minute the old man is sleeping again, chest going up and down.

Alvin listen to the air coming out of the old man's nose making a whistling sound. Some time the whistle is high, sometime is low. Sometime the breathing seem to stop all together. It is while he is listening to this strange windy music that it occur to Alvin. Maybe Papa Chin have a ilk too and maybe he know what to do about it.

Corinthians Thirteen
Thirteen

Is on a Saturday that she first see the man drinking at the standpipe—the dirtiest man she ever see in her whole entire life!

He stand up side of the pipe, rocking back as though he is slightly drunk. When he see her, he immediately start struggling to take off his hat. It take him some time for he don't seem able to use his hands properly. Once he manage to fiddle the hat off, the straight hair flop out and lie like a string of small dead lizards down his back, for it is all twisted up and greasy. No question though that it is straight hair, so she know she is looking at a dirty white man.

The man clearly never hear her walking up to the standpipe. When he succeed in removing the hat, he give a small bow and say, "Howdy, young miss." That is when Angie realize that she been standing still staring at him since her first sight of him suck-sucking his drink of water.

The standpipe is across the road from Maranatha Temple. There is no actual temple yet, just a big sign and a big, big tent, so big, it could hold three, four, maybe even five of the little dwellings in the yard on Mountain Vista Avenue.

Now Friendship Road is not a very long road, and, apart from the Maranatha Temple tent in the middle opposite the standpipe, the big Cameron house at one corner, the big Seaton house at the other, and a couple of smaller houses squeezing up together at each end of the road, it is taken up mostly by big open lands. Except that the said lands are in fact covered with lignum vitae trees, prickly pear and dildo cactus and various kinds of bush, plenty of them with big macca—prickles like the ones Angie imagine the soldiers plaited into a crown and stuck into Jesus's head.

Angie know, for Miss Nella has said it over and over, that she is to stay in sight of the houses, isn't to loiter on her way past the open lands, and if she find herself alone on the road with a boy more than ten years old, or a man of any age at all, she is to walk fast to the nearest house, open the gate as though that is where she live, and walk boldly inside.

Miss Nella say this for her safety's sake but Angie feel that it is maybe a little too much. She not looking for trouble, but she not out to give herself any either. All like today, Saturday, when it is eight o'clock in the morning and everybody working gone to work and everybody else sleeping late, apart from this raggedy man, it is really only she at the standpipe with her two big plastic bottles to fill. She figure long time that she can outrun almost anybody, and if it come to that, she will drop what she is carrying so she can run faster. Besides which she don't intend to "walk boldly" into any gate and run the risk of any bad dog eating her alive.

What is truly concerning her though is that here she is about to catch water at the standpipe after she just witness this very dirty man putting his mouth over the pipe and sucking down water as if is weeks since he taste any.

Well, Angie figure, as she stand there trying to size up the man, at least he make some kind of greeting.

So she nod to him businesslike and reply, "And howdy to yourself, sir," in her best Miss Nella tones. Then she step past him, open the pipe, take the first spurts of water and carefully wash off the pipe-mouth, fill the two bottles, close them up with stoppers, nod leave-taking to the man, turn in the direction of Mountain Vista and begin her journey home.

She take only a few steps when the man call to her.

"You live around here, Miss?"

She stop and consider. She decide since there is nothing forward in the question, it is rude not to answer him. Also it make no sense to say no since otherwise what is she doing catching water at the standpipe? And furthermore it will be a lie and she can't stand people that tell lies.

"Just down the road," she say, facing him. Then she add for insurance, "Everybody round here know me. And what about yourself?"

She surprise when she hear herself asking the question.

The man is still standing in the same place beside the standpipe. He tilt his head to one side, raise his eyebrows a little, and fix his eyes on the ground a short way out in front of him. Angie look at the ground to see if there is something she is missing but it is only the bare dirt as far as she can make out.

"Used to live here one time, Miss. A long time ago."

He sound sort of sad but it is not her business.

"Well I gone now, sir."

She set off again, hurrying to make up for the time she spend talking. As she is walking up the short rise at the end of Friendship Road to where it meet up with Mountain Vista, she is thinking to herself that she have to tell Miss Nella about how the man put his mouth on the pipe. Suppose he is sick? Suppose he have some really terrible disease? She comfort herself that Miss Nella will know what to do.

Then it strike her that if she tell Miss Nella, Miss Nella will inquire whether she was there alone with the man, and she will have to say yes, and Miss Nella not going to be pleased, and she, Angie, will get some kind of punishment, and today is Saturday, the one day Angie get a bit of free time to play with her friend Nola. Angie make up her mind to keep her own counsel. After all, to not say something is not to tell a lie. And besides, the man is not from these parts so he probably not going to be around for long. Since Miss Nella is not likely to ask her for any account, she don't have to give one. If Miss Nella ask her, now, that is another matter.

The thought make her move faster and she manage the corner quick-quick, cross the road and hurry her steps down to number 114 Mountain Vista Avenue—114 A, B, C, D, E, F, G and H, for all the various dwellings in the yard. Angie live at 114 H in a small-small two-room house with Miss Nella and her one real daughter, Francine. Though Angie is not Miss Nella's blood, she don't feel any way about Francine. She know that when she was two years old, her mother, Pansy, take a plane to New York in the hope of getting a job there, leaving Angie with Miss Nella who is as good as a relative by reason of the fact that she know Pansy's mother and grandmother from ages for they all came from a tiny town in St James parish named Mount Moriah.

She, Angie, don't have the slightest recollection of Pansy.

As it happen, the man is at the standpipe the next day, Sunday, and the next, Monday, which is a holiday, Adult Suffrage Day. However, at each of these times there is at least one other person collecting water and, as well, the man keep his distance, standing back from the road on the side across from the tent, minding his own business. Angie nod to him once when she see him looking at her. She not going to be rude but she not encouraging any conversation neither.

When she reach back home the Monday morning, two of Miss Nella's friends are on her doorstep engaged in a war. Angie is not surprised when she see the two warriors. She hear Sister Gertie's mouth well before she swing into the yard. It is the biggest mouth of anybody that she know: Sister Gertie is always glad to explain that the loudness result from thirty years as a primary school teacher during which her classroom was in a gigantic hall containing seven classes, each class divided from the other by nothing but a blackboard.

"So my vocal powers were cultivated," she would say, shouting to prove the point, "in order to make myself heard."

This morning her remarks are jostling the shrill comments of another church sister, Sister May, with both of them ignoring Miss Nella's pat-pattings of the air, signalling them to keep their voices down. Sister May's voice is thinner and higher pitched and she speak in a peculiar accent that she claim is from when she was living in New York. Between her and Sister Gertie there is the squealing and growling you would hear if a bulldog was to get into a pigpen.

Miss Nella is saying nothing at all.

Angie approaching with her water bottles see a head emerge from the apartment next door. She hear Sigismund, a night watchman who live with his baby-mother, Sandra, and two small children, and who is accustomed to come off his shift at six in the morning, holler, "Man trying to sleep. Oonoo can't go somewhere else with the commotion?"

Sigismund know better than to come with any cursing for Miss Nella mind his children when he and their mother are at work. But Miss Nella is a fair person, and the man is not the only one in the yard that need his sleep, so she have no choice but to do what she don't want to, which is invite the two ladies inside and offer them some refreshment. Not that Miss Nella is mean but she know if she give Sister Gertie and Sister May half a chance, they will eat up her whole morning.

The pair make their way inside and sit down on the two little straight-back chairs in the bedroom. Miss Nella sit on the bed. Angie follow them through the door, holding the bottles high up so she can pass between the two of them. She offer a quick greeting—"Morning Sister Gertie; Morning, Sister May"—and slip into the next room where she, Angie, sleep on a small folding bed and where they prepare their food and eat. When she is home on her day off, Francine sleep with Miss Nella in the double bed in the one shrink-down bedroom.

"I tell you, is a disgrace—" Sister Gertie break off to ask Angie, "and how is your God-blessed mother, child?"

"Fine, thank you, Sister Gertie, when last she write."

Now everybody say Angie's mother was the kindest young woman in Vineyard Pen. Some of Miss Nella's friends say as they watch her cook or clean, "That child don't just look like Pansy, she is good-natured same way."

Every time some other person make this comment Angie think, "Not good-natured enough to stay and raise me, though."

She don't know her mother, this Pansy that everybody so love and say she so resemble. She know she live in New York and send money to look after her and clothes and presents for Christmas and her birthday but Miss Nella's face is the first face she remember and in her secret heart she call Miss Nella "Mother dearest". Miss Nella say that one day Pansy will send for her to come and live in New York but Angie not sure she is going, for this Pansy is not anybody that she know.

Sister Gertie start up again.

"Audrey come home and tell me what the man doing and I make sure and go and see it with my own two eye."

She reach out to take the glass of lemonade that Angie just pour from a red Thermos and as she pause to say, "Tanks, Angie," and take a sip of the drink, Sister May seize her opportunity.

Angie don't like Sister Gertie's daughter much. She is stuck-up and interfering and Sister Gertie would die of heart attack if she hear some of the things that came out of Audrey's mouth. Also, though Sister Gertie is very black and forever saying how she is proud to be a African, Angie notice that she clearly think that she has come by something special in Audrey's soft hair and light complexion.

"But after is not you alone see him, Gertie. The thing

is, he sneak and do it. He know is not the right thing. He know it is a shocking thing to do. Not anything you would ever see in a civilized place like New York, for sure."

Sister May's voice get higher as she speak and splinter on "New York, for sure". Angie listen from the next room as she pour water in the kettle, catch up the fire in the coal pot and put the kettle on, for she decide this is the way to deal with the dirty water.

Sister May make a coughing sound and a choking sound. The noise mercifully stop as Miss Nella instruct Sister May to drink some water, telling her to sip slowly.

"Sister May need anything more?"

Angie put her head through the doorway to inquire but Miss Nella tell her they have things under control, so she go back inside to fold away her bed.

Miss Nella now take charge. She never raise her voice but when she talk everybody take notice.

"Any of you see this man put his mouth on the tap?" She don't forget what Sister Gertie say. She just making sure.

Sister May look take time and say, "Well I never really see him."

"Well, I most forsuredly did!" Sister Gertie bat Sister May's fandangled accent out of the way. "I hide behind the ackee tree in the Dunker yard and I my very self see him. I wasn't close, but I see well enough."

Sister Gertie pause as if she is waiting for comments but nobody say anything.

"And I don't make no time pass," she continue. "Right that very minute I go and tell Pastor Huckleby that it is his duty to do something about it, for is all of we without running water that using that standpipe, people with children, and so on. And he say he will talk to the man next time he see him, since it appear that nobody don't know where to find him."

Sister May is still slurping her water.

"Is a light-skin man, you know," Sister Gertie reflect. "Hair straight like ruler, nose fine like needle. Him should know better. I have it in mind that I know him..."

She look off in the distance as she say this.

Sister May open her eyes wide in surprise and ask, "You could know somebody like that, Gertie?"

"If you must know, I am acquainted with plenty white people. You think Pastor is the only white man I know?"

"Is not that I mean at all," Sister May object. "I mean if you could know somebody that behave like that."

Miss Nella listen very quietly to all of this, then she put another question.

"If he is always there at the standpipe, then he must live around here somewhere. Nobody know where he live?"

Angie think she have an idea but she can't say anything of course. She tiptoe close to the doorway. Sister May and Sister Gertie look at each other, then at Miss Nella. They raise their brows and purse their lips, turning them up to their noses so they look like pig snouts, and then together they shake their heads to say no.

"Well," Miss Nella say, "I going to find that out."

"But that don't have anything to do with anything, Nella."

Sister Gertie tuning up again when there is a rap near the bottom of the door. Miss Nella open it to show a little girl standing outside with a large plastic bag in one hand, the other gripping her younger brother.

Miss Nella smile and take the bag and say, "Ah, Melba and Winston. Come in, please, and say 'Good morning' to these ladies..." which the children promptly do then vanish into Angie's charge in the next room.

Miss Nella come back to Sister May and Sister Gertie.

"My sisters, I don't mean to run you, but you see my day's work is starting."

Though it is a holiday Sigismund is working his usual night shift so he can get double time, which mean he have to get his day-sleep, and Sandra is taking the day to visit her mother in the country. Miss Nella therefore babysitting like it is a ordinary day.

The chair squeak as Sister Gertie rise. She start for the door and Sister May follow, of necessity slow, for Sister Gertie have to pick her way around the bed sake of her size.

"I don't think it going to be too hard to sort this out," Miss Nella say as she see them out. "Maybe by service this evening."

"Okay, Nella." Sister May seem glad of any solution. "Whatever you think best," and she wave goodbye at

Angie with her kerchief as she squeeze past Sister Gertie and go out the door ahead of her.

Sister Gertie is not happy. She turn back to study Miss Nella and make as if to say something, but think better of it and continue on out. *She* don't notice Angie nor say any farewell as she march through the door.

Miss Nella wave the two ladies off, promising, "See you tonight at meeting. I saving a seat for you."

There is a joy, joy, joy, joy,
Down in my heart,
Down in my heart,
Down in my heart.
There is a joy, joy, joy, joy,
Down in my heart,
And I want to share it with you.

Sister Gertie and Sister May, late as always even for the late-starting service, are just now making their way up the centre passageway looking for Miss Nella who is always early and so always seated near the front close to the aisle. When Miss Nella see them she move down in the row into the seats she been saving so that they can sit in the end seats. She keep an empty seat between herself and Angie, though, for she is still holding one for Francine.

Sister May slide into her place swiftly and join in the chorus right away. However, Sister Gertie first take off her cardigan, drape it over the back of the seat, adjust her hat, pat her hair, make a wave all around to her paseros in the tent, and then sit down and set to singing.

The chorus is nearly finished.

I have the peace that passeth understanding,
Down in my heart,
And I want to share it with you.

As Reverend Huckleby enters, the choir, robed in bright blue, turn towards him extending their arms palms upward in welcome. The congregation rise.

"Good evening, brothers and sisters. I am sure God will love you so much the better, after that rousing chorus."

This is Reverend Huckleby greeting them from the lectern.

"Good evening, pastor," they respond, making a quiet chuckle for Reverend Huckleby has often preached that the love of God is constant and unchanged by anything they do.

"Please be seated."

It is November and dark outside. There are no streetlights on the road except for the one on the sidewalk near to the standpipe. Apart from that light, and those in the tent, there is deep country night outside. Inside is a different matter. Tent or no tent, the plentiful lights inside are proudly electric, as is the organ, as are the powerful loudspeakers, for Rev Huckleby don't come from the United States for nothing. The generator supplying the tent is his pride and joy.

"Our text for this evening," the pastor begin, opening his large black leather-bound Bible, "is taken from Paul's first letter to the Corinthians, chapter thirteen."

There is a rustling throughout the tent as people open Bibles and look for the chapter. Miss Nella find her place quick-quick. While the others are still shuffling pages, she craning her neck to look down into the back of the tent.

"Who you looking for, Nella?" Sister May whisper in American.

"No that girl, Francine," Miss Nella murmur back. "Mrs Cameron give her the evening off so she should be here long time ago."

Stragglers are still coming in as they are accustomed to do for the first half-an-hour of the service.

"Come in brothers and sisters and little ones. Early or late, all are welcome."

It take a little while for everybody to settle in, for mothers to hush babies, for grown-ups to find their Bibles and then hiss at the older children, "Look on the pictures in the picture books-them, no?" Bible story picture books are provided for reading, tearing and eating.

The Reverend resume.

"Many new Christians, frightened by the size of the Bible, come to me and ask if I can't sum it up for them. They say they are simple people, just like the people Jesus taught, so they know he must have left some short and straightforward teaching that is central to the Good News of salvation."

He pause and look around to make sure of silence and complete attention.

"The chapter we consider this evening could be said to offer us such a summary."

Sister May have her hand up in front of her face as she whisper to Sister Gertie, passing on Miss Nella's worry about Francine. When she look up she see Reverend Huckleby looking straight at her. Same time hand drop and mouth shut like a manhole closing. Angie smile to herself for although Sister May is a big somebody, the guilty look on her face is just the same as how Winston and Melba look when Miss Nella catch them doing what they are not supposed to do.

"Please read with me chapter thirteen, in particular, verses seven and thirteen." Silence is still reigning, so the Reverend is pleased to continue.

"Verse seven tells us, 'Love bears all things, believes all things, hopes all things, endures all things.' And verse thirteen sums up—notice that it is Corinthians thirteen thirteen, so you can remember easily—verse thirteen says, 'So faith, hope, love abide, these three; but the greatest of these is love.'"

As if on cue, the second the Reverend say this, a scream to wake the deadest duppy arise from right outside the back of the tent, a piercing cry, seasoned with bad words. The whole congregation twist in their chairs as the scream get louder.

Angie catch sight of a figure behaving in a manner the like of which she never behold before. The man enter the tent rubbing his eyes with both hands. He trip over the electric wires connected to the sound and lighting equipment, stumble into the chairs left empty for late-comers at the ends of the last two rows, bounce into the standing mike at the back of the tent where people come to give testimony and knock it down.

The whole heap of noise wake up the babies and they join in his screeching to make a raucous chorus.

People in the rows near to this flapping creature small-up themselves and lean away as far as they can, holding their children close and looking at the man wide-eyed and terrified. He is now stumbling down the centre aisle, as if the bright lights on the platform are drawing him, the foul language now collapsed into mutterings of rage. When he come to the baptismal pool, a large solid plastic structure about two feet deep, filled with water and sunk partway into the ground right below the platform, he bend down clumsy-like, put his face into the water and wash it over and over, then straighten up and plunge his arms in up to the elbow. After he finish these ablutions, he start up the steps, trailing water for his clothes are now dripping wet.

The congregation gasp when the creature wash his face and hands in the pool. Even Reverend Huckleby—a man who has been in Africa and seen gorillas, tigers, lions, elephants and all manner of wild animals—even his mouth drop open. Everybody is startled but Sister Gertie. When Sister Gertie see the man, a smile steal across her face and her eyes shine. The look on her face stay only a short time and she quickly settle back down into Corinthians.

But she not fast enough to escape Miss Nella's eye.

The congregation stare as the man shamble up the stairs onto the platform, groaning softly and wiping his eyes and mouth in turn. He moving towards the lectern that the pastor is hanging onto, and when finally Reverend Huckleby realize what is about to happen, he look to the sides and back of the church and issue a summons.

"Will the ushers approach the platform, please?"

Ushers get unstuck and rush up as the man reach the lectern. Every man jack watch as he stop, slowly take his shirttails and wipe eyes, face and mouth, and push the grubby hat off his head, just managing to catch it as it drop. Then, as if a spirit overtake him, he lift his chin, look square at the pastor and ask in a most cultivated voice—Angie has heard Miss Nella speak of 'cultivated voices'—"May I address the congregation?"

Well, you should see mouth drop again. People in front lean forward and those who are in back stand up to see. Sister Gertie jump up and nearly topple back onto a slim little man behind her. Reverend Huckleby is expecting calamity and instead, this! A fit of throat-clearing take him. His eyes open up and his unfailing patience is about to desert him when Miss Nella rise to her feet and say, her voice carrying clear: "Pastor, please allow the gentleman to speak."

Angie can see Reverend Huckleby is not pleased at Miss Nella's request, but he long ago take the measure of Miss Nella. He signal for the man to come up to the microphone.

"Thank you, sir," the fellow say as he take his place behind the lectern.

"I want to apologize first for my use of bad language in the House of God. However, you will forgive me, in the circumstances. If you stoop to drink a little water and find your mouth on fire, then try to wipe away the pepper heat from your mouth and get so confused that you put that same hand into your eyes, thus inflaming mouth and eyes, you may well say what you shouldn't. I am indeed sorry, in particular because it happened in this place of worship."

The man can clearly handle the English language and the faint American accent not doing no harm. Angie wonder if that is how Miss Nella want her to talk.

"I listened to the pastor's teaching with interest." He address Reverend Huckleby. "I compliment you, sir, on your broadcast systems. I heard every word."

It is a point of pride with the pastor so he allow the seriousness of his face to tone itself down.

"I won't take up much time. I will only say two things. I've traveled in my time, lived abroad, and mixed with rich and poor. In so doing, I have encountered viciousness and ill will. But it is a long time since I've met the pure malice I've encountered here today."

His lips trembling but he take a deep breath and go on.

"Even out in the world, it is said, 'Don't hit a man when he's down.' If you're a Christian, you should do better than those in the world. And if, as your pastor has just said, it's charity that counts with Jesus, then I'm sure that whoever put pepper on the mouth of that standpipe is no Christian."

A ripple run through the congregation but Reverend Huckleby look from left to right and there is quiet. Miss Nella gaze is firmly forward. Sister Gertie's eyes is looking down, only peeping up from under her hat-brim now and then.

"I wish, though, to tell you about two persons I have met here who did treat me like Christians."

Another ripple, and people whispering.

"I have been living in the open land over yonder these past few days," he point across Friendship Road. "I don't propose to say why, but it's with good reason. I've had no food of my own, nor water, nor change of clothes. But I survived by the generosity of a young woman who works in the house beside the open land. She shared her food with me and gave me something to drink, as she was able. I wish to publicly thank her."

Miss Nella still looking steadfastly at the man. Though Angie can't see her face, she is certain Miss Nella is looking proud, since for sure it is Francine that the man is speaking about.

"And I wish also to thank a young miss who came several times to fetch water." Angie get frighten when the man say this. "She answered me when I greeted her and told me that she lived around here when I asked. She was polite and dignified. I would be glad to count her as my own. Her mother should be rightly proud of her."

Angie is not surprised about the part concerning Francine for that is exactly what Francine would do, but this last part is puzzling her. She know that Miss Nella must be wondering who is this child whose mother this man know. Truth to tell, Angie was fearful it was she the man was talking about and worrying that she was going get into trouble with Miss Nella. But since the man don't know either her born-mother or Miss Nella, it can't be she.

"That's it," the man finish up. "I thank you for the opportunity to have my say."

The man walk lopsided across the platform, down the stairs, down the aisle and out into the darkness. While everybody is staring after him, Miss Nella jump up and say to Sister May and Sister Gertie, "I cry excuse, sisters. Please let me pass."

When Angie see Miss Nella get up, she rise too. Sister Gertie start up but Miss Nella fix her with a look.

"Please settle down, brothers and sisters," Reverend Huckleby exhort the congregation. "This has been quite an event, but we need to compose ourselves and remember this is the Lord's house. Sister Nella will know what course of action to take. Ushers, stand by to assist."

Miss Nella is outside now, running after the man, Angie close behind her. He is across the road, right on the edge of the circle of light by the standpipe, about to go through a space in the barbwire fence on his way into the open land.

"Mr Cameron, Mr Cameron!"

Angie is stunned when Miss Nella call the man's name.

He stand up slowly.

"You know me, ma'am?" he ask, facing her. When he look across to the standpipe and see Angie, he smile and say, "How are you this evening, miss?"

"Well, thank you, sir," Angie answer in a voice that get smaller as she speak, for Miss Nella must know from this that she meet the man before.

Miss Nella address Mr Cameron.

"I live here thirty years, sir. When I see you this evening, I know you right away for Mrs Cameron's husband, Miss Celia's father."

"Mrs Cameron's former husband," he correct her.

"You not planning to go back over that open land to sleep tonight?"

"Well, I don't have much choice."

"Reverend Huckleby will not allow that. You can stop

with one of the ushers."

She pause. Angie wait to hear what she will say.

"But maybe you would prefer to stay with Angie and me?"

"With you, ma'am? Are you certain?"

"Quite certain," Miss Nella declare. "You will want to be near to Miss Celia. It is a very small premises, but Angie can sleep with me and so I can offer you a bed and, of course, something to eat. We have no running water but this young lady here," she look at Angie, "is, as I think you know, good at fetching water."

Angie is looking down on the ground. Mr Cameron say, "I'm afraid I don't remember you, ma'am. Please remind me of the name?"

"My name is Nella Vaughn, sir. You don't have occasion to know me but I know a lady who used to work for you and Mrs Cameron. She was Edris Howell. She nurse Miss Celia when she just born."

"I remember Edris very well," Mr Cameron say.

"Angie," Miss Nella talk firm and precise. "Run and tell Elder Matthews that Mr Cameron will stop with us. He will want to know the outcome of this matter."

And Miss Nella set off with Mr Cameron for number 114 H Mountain Vista Road, walking slowly to give Angie time to catch up with them.

Miss Nella is not pleased for Angie is to make sure that they always have water and it is almost finished. Mr Cameron explain that his fingers cannot come together, not even to make a cup to drink water at the standpipe, which is why he put his mouth on it, so he can't lift the plastic containers, but he offer to go with Angie. Miss Nella say it's all right. She instruct Angie to fix Mr Cameron some supper then she step outside and rap on Sigismund and Sandra's door.

Angie pour some hot water from a blue Thermos (red for cold and blue for hot) and make Mr Cameron some cocoa-tea. She open a tin of bully beef and is cutting up onion and Scotch bonnet pepper to make sandwiches.

"I don't suppose you want any pepper, sir?"

Mr Cameron smile halfway.

"No thanks, Angie. Not this evening."

Miss Nella come back with trousers and a shirt that she borrow from Sigismund who just have time to go to the standpipe before he leave for work.

"I hope these will suit, sir," Miss Nella say, handing the clothes to Mr Cameron.

After Mr Cameron wash up and change his clothes, Miss Nella say grace and they start on the sandwiches.

"Pity you never come to someone in the church and tell your trouble, sir. All this would not have to happen."

"You are right, Miss Nella, but pride is a pitiful thing. I hardly expected to be well-received, given the circumstances in which I left, which I daresay you recall?"

"If I ever knew them, sir, I forget long since. I have

plenty of my own concerns, so other people's business have to struggle to find a way onto my list."

"Well, I will remind you."

"No need to do so now, Mr Cameron. There is time enough for that. Angie, you should be in bed long ago. You sleep with me. And please take out a fresh sheet for Mr Cameron."

Angie say goodnight and go into Miss Nella's bedroom to find the sheet, but she listen through the door as Mr Cameron finish his story. He was making his way in a taxi from the airport meaning to try and find a room to rent near their house on Mountain Vista for he decide after the accident that mash up his hands that he would like to come back and see his daughter before anything more happen to him.

With no warning, the taxi pull over to one side and two men jump in the back. The two of them and the driver beat him up so he lose consciousness. When he come to himself he find that they rob his money, documents and suitcase and leave him with only the clothes on his back. He is ashamed to approach anybody with his tear up clothes and his sorrowful tale, so he decide to camp out in the open land hoping to see Celia if she come out in the yard. The first morning he is there, he see Francine when she come down near the fence to hang up washing and he call to her.

Angie just manage to hear the story to the end before she fall asleep.

On Tuesday as day light Miss Nella wake up Angie.

"I am going up to Mrs Cameron, so you have to give Mr Cameron some breakfast and mind Melba and Winston if I don't come back in good time. If you have to miss school, so be it. I will explain to the teacher."

It don't take Miss Nella too long. She come back as Angie is putting sardines picked up with onion and thick slices of brown bread on the table.

"Mr Cameron, sorry to interrupt," she say businesslike as ever. "Francine didn't come to meeting last night because Celia take a bad turn, so you should get up there quick as you can. I tell Mrs Cameron you are here and she not grinning at the news but she say you may come and see your child."

His face look green as he stop eating and rise from the table.

"I will go now, Miss Nella, though I don't know how I can face Mrs Cameron, nor what I will say to my daughter."

"Miss Celia know you come a long way to see her, sir. And if you speak from the heart, that will most likely do. I will come with you for Francine been up all night and I promise Mrs Cameron to relieve her so she can get some sleep."

When Miss Nella reach back home at seven o'clock that evening she is well tired. She tell Angie that all day Mr Cameron sit quiet beside the bed when Celia is sleeping and when she wake he tell her stories about New York. Poor Mrs Cameron spend the day trying to find out if Celia must go back in the hospital and if the worst is soon to happen.

Shortly after Miss Nella take off her hat and sit down to drink a cup of mint tea, they hear the sound of shoes scraping on the front door mat.

"Come in, Gertie," Miss Nella raise her voice just enough so that it carry to the door. "It's open. Come through to the dining table. Is where we are."

"Good evening, Nella." Sister Gertie's voice is not quite as loud as usual. She enter and sit.

"Angie here too, Gertie," Miss Nella say.

"Evening, Angie my love. Sorry for bad manners. I am somewhat distracted."

"What is distracting you, Gertie?"

"I not accustomed to being summoned like a child, Nella."

"Angie," Miss Nella say, "Run next door and see if Sandra need a little help with the children."

Angie know why Miss Nella say this, but, much as she want to stay, there is nothing to do but what she is told. One comfort though: she know she will hear Sister Gertie's part of the conversation coming through, loud and clear.

So said, so done.

"I am not a woman to tell lies, Nella. Yes, I put the Scotch bonnet pepper on the pipe. It was my bounden duty."

Angie rap on Sigismund and Sandra's door. No answer.

"I not sorry. He deserve anything he get. That man is not a decent man, abandon not one but two woman, one pregnant, one with young baby, sake of his base and disgusting lust."

Angie rap again, louder. She is still hearing Sister Gertie at full throttle.

"How I know is two woman? It matter how I know? Come back like a mangy dog, living in the bush like a common criminal. Which is bad, but since it don't affect nobody else, so be it. But to be reckless with other people's health and safety, to contaminate the pipe that all of we fetch water from?"

Still nobody come to answer Angie's rapping. She decide to go back to Miss Nella's door and wait outside since maybe Sigismund and Sandra and the children will soon come back. When she take up her station, she hear a new voice.

"Gertie, I didn't know. I didn't recognize you..."

Angie is trying to think how Mr Cameron could be inside.

"Because I look like a two-ton truck? Some people pine and get slender; some people feed sorrow. Don't talk to me. You have a nerve to look me in my face. Cast your eyes down, you lecherous pig, you nest of vipers, you...you whited sepulcher!"

"Gertie, I had no idea, I didn't dream—"

"No. You wasn't dreaming. You was wide awake. Riding me like a jackass."

"Gertie, keep your voice down. Small children live in this yard."

"Listen to me, Nella Vaughn, I never invite myself down here. I never intend to have nothing to do with this Revelational beast with seven heads and as many horns on each. After he don't have nothing to give to neither me nor Audrey. Look on him! Him favour some ragamuffin country-come-town!"

"Fathering is more than money, Gertie. He is about to lose one daughter. He need to do right by the next one."

"Leave mi pikni out of this!"

"As for you, Mr Cameron," Angie frighten when she hear this voice from Miss Nella for it is cold as ice, "you best tell us if you was the Vineyard Pen village ram and we are to expect to see a long line of fatherless children once word get out that you are here?"

Angie still trying to understand when she hear Melba and Winston laughing and see Sigismund and his family come round the corner of their house. She hasten to greet them, for she know if Miss Nella find her outside without a good reason, she in plenty trouble. When she inside and settling down to read the children a story, she can't hear Miss Nella nor Mr Cameron but she can still hear Sister Gertie.

"Me? Forgive you? Your wife can forgive you. Her child can forgive you. All Audrey can forgive you if she want, but as for me, Gertie Samuels, Jesus self would have to descend and instruct me to forgive you for what you do to me and my child."

So there it was. Plain as day. It stop Angie in the middle of a sentence, mouth open to pronounce the next word.

"Angie? Angie!"

"Angie, what happen to you? I must call Mama?"

When she realize that she is at a full stop listening like a watchdog to a foreign sound, she start to read so fast Melba complain she can't hear the words properly.

A good half an hour later Miss Nella stick her head through the door and say, "Angie, you can come back over. Mr Cameron and me going up the road with Sister Gertie. We soon come back."

Is nearly midnight before Angie hear Miss Nella take her key and open the door, for Angie know she is to lock it after a certain hour. She long since finish eating supper, putting on her nightie and settling into Miss Nella's bed.

She listen as Miss Nella come in, lock the door, put away one and two things in the next room, check to see everything is secure, then come into the bedroom and start getting ready for bed. She know that she can't ask Miss Nella about Mr Cameron and Sister Gertie but she think she understand a little about the pepper on the pipe, about why Sister Gertie is so proud of Audrey's complexion and soft hair, maybe even about why Audrey's mouth is so nasty.

It is not so simple, not so simple at all.

Crucial Concern

Sunday. Hold-and-Haul (everybody called him H&H) and Simey were beating their brains out to find out who had insprignated Miss Rosie Messias's one-daughter, Isolyn. It was really more H&H's obsession, sucking on his brain like a flea on the back of the last surviving dog.

H&H swore it was Delgado, Delgado being Miss Rosie's man.

"Is a thing happen in this country all the time," he observed, sagely. "Those crufty old men just take advantage of young girls. The girl children afraid to tell their mother, for the mother not going to believe them—don't want to believe them. Next thing you know another girl pikni walking round behind a big belly and she not saying nothing, for fear her mother throw her out."

Simey made no reply to this diatribe, which was not usual for him.

"So why you screwing up your face so, Simey?" H&H inquired. "You don't think is Miss Rosie's man?"

"No" said Simey, and proceeded to accuse H&H of being bad-minded.

Isolyn's pregnancy was the first thing that ever made them think further forward in their lives than plans for the very immediate future—say, the next few hours or, at a pinch, the next day. True, they counted on some things, Isolyn and Miss Rosie being two. But H&H decided to say nothing further on the subject of Isolyn for it seemed like Simey was having a day when he was 'frownish'.

He had days like that from time to time and H&H dealt with his mood by holding down on the talking and laughing, never mind that when they were ready, nobody was better than the two of them at romping and carrying-on. If you have only today, the one way to get through is romp and carry on.

Now if you looked at it one way, the pregnancy business concerned neither of them, but if you looked at it another way, it was a matter of crucial concern, for by means of Isolyn, their long-time buddy, they were connected to a key spot, that being Miss Rosie's kitchen. It was a small kitchen, a little slapped-together affair appurtenanced to the rear of Miss Rosie's cold supper shop. But size-of-kitchen determineth not quality-of-bickle, and, sake of Isolyn's kind offices, the makeshift kitchen put a decent distance between the two of them and hungry belly many a time.

Consequently, anything bad for Miss Rosie's one-daughter was bad for the two of them. And this baby-making business was a very serious thing. Isolyn was very bright, doing good-good in school. She was intending, the good Lord permitting, to do nursing after her end-of-school exams. But now that somebody 'fall her', it seemed all such plans would have to be discarded.

This Sunday morning H&H and Simey were warming up a concrete wall by Hannis Trace and Pink Lane corner. Eleven o'clock rang out by the Parish Church bell and everything was quiet as the grave. There was not a soul in the vicinity to make any trouble, for back of the wall on the two sides of Hannis Trace was an enormous concrete dump, what was left of some old factories that the authorities bulldozed so no criminals could take refuge there. At least that was what Babylon, a.k.a. Her Majesty's Constabulary Force, said, and then proceeded to knock them down with not the slightest regard for the person or persons to whom the property belonged. The upshot was that there was nothing going on in the pile of rubble and concrete, nothing harboured there except some vicious pieces of broken glass-bottle, capable of shredding your foot-bottom to bits.

As for Pink Lane, that was likewise a wasteland, from 80s time. Two different political party offices, one Labourite and one Socialist, used to face each other across Pink Lane right on the Hannis Trace corner. H&H's mother's father—himself shot to death in crossfire three years before—had told him that when party politricks started in Jamaica, two cousins used to control that side of Kingston. When the Labourite cousin was sitting in Parliament, the Socialist cousin was constituency caretaker; when the Socialist cousin was sitting, the Labourite cousin was caretaking. They would lend each other money when things were tough and send over a case of beer if one of them came into some extra funds from lottery or racehorse, drop pan or peaka-pow. So it suited the two of them very well to have the two offices regarding each other across the road.

Then *somebody* brought guns. And drugs. And that was the end of that. Nobody knew who that *somebody* might be. So far as Johnny-Public could see—so said H&H's Grampa—it never suited the two cousins, for their business was running too well on the cross-the-road arrangement. Some said it was the CIA. Some said the KGB. Some said the Mafia. Some said Big Time Drug Runners. Nobody was exactly sure just who, but whoever they were, they perpetrated their evil well indeed. Two weeks before the 1980 election, the two party offices burned down, one today, the other one tomorrow. Four people died in the fires and thirty-two people died in the subsequent five days in the vicinity of that corner.

Between the fires and Babylon's flattening the buildings on Hannis Trace, then, the entire district was a no-man's-land, a graveyard of discarded old cars and sundry piles of rubbish.

A dump as safe as a church.

"Pow-pow. Pow-pow. Pow-pow-pow."

The noises, not nearby but not that far away, made them jump and turn to look at each other.

"No problem, man." H&H grinned. "Just some old car back-firing."

He took a sip of beer and passed the bottle to Simey.

It hadn't escaped their notice that somebody had recently decorated the wall. As he leaned back, H&H glanced at the bright new squiggles and observed, "Human being idle you know."

"My Granny say, 'Idle man's brain is Satan's workshop'." Simey nodded in agreement. "Satan must be was apprenticing a couple devils right there."

The wall in question displayed a set of ominous inscriptions: "Death to the Uncommitted"; "Lackeys of the Backra Oppressor Shall Perish by Black Hands"; "We ABBREVIATE Fence-Sitters"; "Fire for the Politically Apathetic and the Socially Unconscious". The said tidings were proclaimed as being "Signed by Politically Conscious Functionally Literate Youth".

Hold-and-Haul and Simey were not in either the PC or the FLY category. Their mothers had promoted a somewhat different life experience by freeing them early from the burden of formal schooling in order to undertake the breadwinning pursuits of begging and washing windshields when they were, respectively, eight and nine years old.

This was also how, a long time ago, the two of them met and, after a couple altercations over who was invading whose corner, teamed up. Thereafter the partnership had extended its undertakings to selling mangoes, june plums, otahiti apples, guineps and other fruit captured from the Botanical Gardens, the University of the West

Indies campus, the Faith Cancer Hospice, or on the occasions when supplies in these locations proved inadequate, any other available trees.

H&H was in charge of supplies while Simey was the face card, for he was born with the gift of the gab and a cherubic countenance that could charm the last penny from an old lady's purse.

They had become successful enough at their trades, which they continued to ply, but all three (selling fruit, begging, washing car windows) had their good and bad seasons, and right now at the start of the year, it being pretty much off season because of the ravages of Christmas, a free plate of soup from Miss Rosie's shop would serve to banish gas from empty bellies.

In their efforts at survival, they assuredly benefited from the ministrations of two over-achieving guardian angels. Never mind that they earned a living on the streets, they had never ever come up against a serious threat to life or person. Maybe it also helped that the very same vigilant mothers who put them to work as mere babes also kindly extended them a caution.

"Court house expensive, eh? And the hottest room in hell is better than a jail cell in this town. So just stay well clear of trouble. You understand?"

Experience is the best teacher. When they first started the begging business, every couple weeks or so some somebody armed with a knife held them up.

"Hi, little youth. Hold on right there. The Big Man

here—" said without regard for the actual size of the robber in question, "feel say that you two sprats need to make a donation to a worthy cause."

Pause, then laughter, followed by the announcement: "Me."

They always handed over the money giggling like idiots, at first from sheer terror and after that because it clearly worked in their favour. They giggled, looked foolish, and made a hasty getaway as soon as the immediate danger was past. Indeed, one mugger, taken with his young victims, kindly returned some of their money.

"Take this. Two of you better fill your belly before you go home to take licks from your mother because you come back with your two hand empty."

It took them a while but soon they had worked up a strategy to deal with worthy causes. First, they didn't beg on any corner two days running. Then they hid the beg-money in small bags that they stuffed into two larger sacks—of manure. When anyone accosted them, they quickly opened the sacks full of dung.

"Manure, sir. See?"

The crook inevitably retired as the two of them advanced, each opening a foul-smelling bag. "We gather it fresh from the open land in the morning and we sell to the rich ladies-them to use to grow flowers."

The manure proved an effective deterrent. If any bandit suspected that it contained treasure, none ever put his hand in to find it.

By the time they reached their teens (by then both mothers had gone off to seek their fortunes in foreign lands), they knew how to locate a good base from which to operate: any church with a soup kitchen, Xaymaca Save the Children, the YMCA, the YWCA, Women's Crisis Centre, and so on. A base provided important things: a pipe to drink water from, people that got to know you and could tell Babylon that you were not worthless, and a refuge if anybody was chasing you for any reason.

True, they still had to make a donation every few months, if they were caught with spoils that had not made it into the manure bags, but they figured they could live with that. For the rest, they stayed far from trouble, which after six years on the street they could smell quick enough to be ready for it.

So apart from knowing the local top rankings by name, by reputation and by sight from a safe distance, neither of them had any real acquaintance with truly unruly, outrightly criminal, wantonly murderous types. And since nobody, criminal or otherwise, had laid claim to the place where they now were, it had become a habit for the two of them to cotch up on that corner to reason, share a cigarette, or split a hot-hops. In time they came to think that the corner belonged to them.

Upon this Sunday, then, buoyed up by peace if not by plenty, the young entrepreneurs were entertaining not the slightest suspicion that the very fact of their backsides polishing the colourful squiggles on the wall might provoke a single living soul, since the broad sea of concrete on the Hannis Trace side was at the moment disturbed only by rippling waves of heat caused by a Sunday sun working its way up into cloudless blue.

"POW-POW."

A ugly noise exploded from behind the top of the wall. H&H and Simey dropped to the ground, rolling up into two balls. They remained thus, motionless like the faithful arrested at the final trumpet-call waiting for Judgement—which is what to their certain knowledge gunshots brought.

It seemed like eternity, but King Jesus didn't appear. Eventually, H&H took his time, tilted his chin forward and peeped up.

On top of the wall, he saw a perfect set of white teeth with a red-brown head around them behind a large hand holding a small black lethal item, the whole picture set against the bluest sky. H&H wasn't sure he was seeing right but he decided that half a warm beer couldn't so humbug his understanding.

The mouth in the red-brown moon-face started to move; it made sounds like a drain swallowing dirty water in a hurry.

"Look here, Buss-eye..." it glugged.

H&H thought he recognized face and voice.

"Is Feelgood, Dr Feelgood," he muttered to Simey in a whisper, "Toppest ranking ganja don above Slipe Pen Road."

"Just look on the two piece of dry codfish obstructing the new-brand inscription that conscious youth establish on this wall." Dr Feelgood pointed to the writing on the wall.

The eyes of both young men flew to the wall and saw again the scrawling shapes: they could imagine no meaning to the writing that might put them in any danger at all.

Then another head reached the top of the wall. Blue-black skin this time, head shaved smooth like Isaac Hayes and large dark glasses under bushy eyebrows. The lethal item this head was brandishing wasn't small. Since H&H and Simey were not experienced in the matter of weapons, neither knew what kind of gun it was. But for certain it could kill not one-one but plenty people at a time—any fool could see that.

"Is what make the little winjy youth-them so fool that them hiding poor people proclamations? Is play them playing with them life?"

This sound was deep, rich and soft, like it should have been singing old-time love tunes in a tuxedo and black tie. It presumably belonged to "Buss-eye", but he was not a ranking or even a lieutenant that either of them recognized.

Dr Feelgood laughed a long laugh, swirling more dirty water down his throat.

"What you say, Buss-eye? Me take one backside, you take the next one?"

By now, H&H was snatching for every prayer he had ever heard, throwing up the bits and pieces as they came.

"Gentle Jesus, meek and mild... forgive us as we forgive our trespassers... Now I lay me down to sleep..."

As for Simey, he made a promise, if God spared life, that he would look after Isolyn and make sure she finished her studies and take a deep and continuing interest in her, and Miss Rosie, and most of all the baby on the way.

Next minute all hell broke loose. The big gun and the small gun started barking from the top of the wall. Bullets were flying across Pink Lane as if Armageddon had come.

Simey and H&H moved past one another like someone had lit a fire in their tails. H&H took off up Hannis Trace like the Devil was at his back while Simey went up Pink Lane like a duppy army was chasing him.

Well, Hannis Trace is a long track. Old cars block it, gullies cut across it. So when H&H pushed the gate of Miss Rosie's premises at Church Street and Ivy Green, Simey had reached the cold supper shop long since. The Parish Church clock was striking twelve, and all H&H wanted was some cool water and a safe place to sit down. And some lunch.

When he pushed the door of the kitchen, he saw four people. He saw Delgado standing up to one side in a nonchalant kind of pose, the kind that was supposed to say you are by-standing when in fact you are taking a keen interest. Delgado was sipping something from a glass so long and wet that it made H&H's mouth-water run.

But what was otherwise going on in the kitchen was stunning enough that it made him forget his thirst.

Miss Rosie had one hand in Simey's collar and was backing him up against the Dover stove and waggling a very big finger from the other hand in his face. Isolyn, serene as you please, was sitting at the table, one hand patting the small bump of her belly, one pleased-as-puss smile playing around her mouth.

And it was when he see who Isolyn was regarding with a look of the tenderest affection that H&H got a clue.

In truth, he felt a bit ashamed, for Isolyn's gaze was not for Delgado. He also felt somewhat vexed, for all this time he had been thinking Isolyn liked him better than she liked Simey. He supposed in all truth he had to admit that, as Simey would say, "There is like, and then there is *like*."

It was when Miss Rosie stopped, looked at him and said, "Catching flies, H&H? For none are in this kitchen..." that he realized his mouth was still open, and he clapped it shut.

"I see things working out," H&H said to Isolyn as he took his time picking his way across to the table, and pulled out a chair and sat down.

"We will see what we will see," Isolyn said, soft, like the Sphinx.

And when H&H thought about it, he figured things hadn't just worked out, they had worked out for the best.

Under no circumstances would Miss Rosie see her daughter's baby-father go without good food and shelter. So Simey was set. As for him, if he played his cards right, they would ask him to stand up for the baby at the christening. Without a doubt, from time to time—say, when he came to visit his god-child—without a doubt, a caring god-father could have a taste of whatever morsels were in Miss Rosie's pot.

Blood

Ainsley can't let go of the shame about Sharon and the knife business. Every minute as his foot pumping, pumping, he try to forget the edge of the blade against Sharon's soft skin, the feel of her neck-string pushing up against it and slacking off, as her full breasts rise and fall. Right in the womb of his mind is a feeling that terrify him more than anything. He know he like the power, the knowledge that if his hand move, that soft neck would get cut and blood would flow. No mind how he try, he can't get his brain around that at all.

But now is not the time for any philosophical business. He jump over two big stones which the last heavy rain bring down into a track that is a river of small white stones, hard on his foot-bottom even though he have on shoes.

The reason he have the knife is because he need a weapon. Of course, he never use one yet, neither gun, cutlass, whip, not even a switchblade, for he never in his life use force against another human being. But the types that traffic in weed and crack and heroin and cocaine and God know what else don't make fun. And when Sharon wouldn't answer him, well, is like some other person take over his body and start talk out of his mouth.

And he expect better from Sharon. If she care about Duarte, why she never answer the question he ask her right away as he ask it?

His mind run on his mother.

"Bad luck worse than obeah," Mama used to say.

His heart sore when he think of his mother. He consider the plenty bad luck in her life. Two sons dead. Husband gone long time. And she so mad she hardly know Ainsley when he visit her in the sanatorium, bring her a few tins of sardine, a couple soaps. Nothing much, for he don't really have much, and besides, Ainsley know if Mama get to eat one sardine, use one soap out of what he bring for her, she lucky.

Now his little brother get mix up with a serious don and carrying a gun. Duarte, Mama's wash-belly, the one she love can't finish. Ainsley know that if anything happen to Duarte, it going to kill Mama for sure.

Mama never tell anybody the whole story but Ainsley remember when he was four, just starting to go to basic school, he remember a big commotion late-late one night. If he close his eye—if he close his eye he break his bloody neck! All of a sudden the track turn steep-steep. If he don't watch where he is going he good to trip and tumble the whole way down. And just as well he start paying attention, for next minute he see a dead dog stretch the whole way across and he barely in time to jump over the stinking mess of intestines and nyam-away meat. He hear wings flapping and glance up to see a army of John Crows circling in the sky.

When the slope ease off a bit, Ainsley mind take off again, back to that night. He can see Raymond and Fenton jumping up in the bed—is one big bed that the three of them sleep in—then jumping down and running to the door, for it was only them and Mama in the house. Five days before that, Papa leave for Haiti on a shopping trip. He never come back.

He hear Raymond and Fenton go outside. They stay a long time. He start to feel fraid, start to feel that something gone wrong, and he sit up and rub his eye, and he decide he going to see for himself. Just as he getting down off the big old four-poster, holding onto the sheet and sliding himself down, Raymond bustle back in the room.

"What happen Ainsley? You dream something bad? Is all right, man. Mama soon come. Go on back in the bed and lie down. Nearly time to get up to go to school."

Next day Mama face swell and her two eye bruise-up. A big white bandage is on her head and she not moving so good. Raymond and Fenton say she get a bad fall. That day he remember his dream. A man is lying on top of Mama, slamming his bottom part against her, pushing something into her body like a stick or a piece of pipe. He have a knife at her throat and when he finish beating her, he arch his back like a lizard.

He don't bother to tell anybody this bad-bad dream for there is trouble enough in the house. He try hard to forget it and in time it go away.

When they get big, Mama tell them what happen that night and is then that Ainsley remember the long ago dream. She say Duarte was a seed a man put in her belly against her will, but once it start grow she couldn't do nothing but carry it and born it. She say she promise God she would love the child, for is half hers anyway, and Psalms say God-self was putting it together and growing it in her womb.

Ainsley could still hear Mama voice.

"Seed catch if Godalmighty will. If I wasn't to carry this child, you think Jehovah can't release it from my belly?"

When the baby born, she call him Duarte for her grandfather that come from Cuba long time ago. She smile broad when she look in the baby wrinkle-up face.

"This boy going to be trouble," she say, "just like my father father. I don't know what kind of trouble, but I know this Duarte pikni is going to raise Cain!"

And talk the truth, Duarte is the funniest thing on two foot, own-mind from the day he drop out of her womb. It don't bother Mama though. Is Ainsley that had a way to flinch when Mama slap Duarte, for Duarte was a tumpa little fellow, solid like pudding, and when her hand-middle connect with Duarte's fat backside, the *ker-plai, ker-plai* sound cause Ainsley to feel it like the licks was raining on his own skin. But Duarte don't cry. Just look on Mama daring-like, straight up in her face, and run away, and when he reach far enough, just turn back and look on her again, laughing his *keh-keh* Anansi laugh.

By the time Mama discover that is not just a pikni the rapist give her, disease eating her soul-case.

The thing is, things happen little by little over such a long time that neither Mama nor anybody she know could figure out what was wrong. First she complain of terrible pains in her belly, then she start to vomit and can't stop. When the home remedies she try don't work, she go to the doctor and they start the tests. Meantime growths coming out on her skin and she losing control of her movements.

Then they hear from the doctor that things gone too far.

"We can't cure syphilis at this stage," the doctor tell Duarte and Ainsley. "The problem is that your mother remained asymptomatic for as long as she did. Now it is a matter of waiting for the inevitable, and there is no way to predict whether that will be a year or ten years."

Is about that time Duarte start going to Toronto every couple of months. Mama still at home struggling to manage with the help of her church sisters. Ainsley doing what he can for her when he not at work. Then her mind start to wander, though she fight hard against it. In the end, it reach the stage where they have no choice. She have to go to St Mary's Hospice, a small annex to the sanitarium where they keep patients that are 'mental'.

When Ainsley talk to Duarte about money, for they don't really have anything much between them, Duarte say that the doctor tell him accommodation for mental patients is free, for government can't have them wandering the streets. Poor foolish Ainsley take Duarte at his word.

The track is nearly flat now and he start looking for the short parochial road that connect to the main road that follow the coastline into Puerto Bueno. It vex him to think that his mother end up dependent on the some-timishness of the hospital staff. When he visit her and she in the worst way and can't help herself at all, can't turn in the bed or call for the bedpan in time, is Ainsley same one sponge down her body and clean her up.

And every time he think, "So what happen when I not here?"

It was only Mama, Duarte and Ainsley left. In '98, police gunfire kill Raymond and Fenton. They not political nor criminal nor nothing like that. Just out in the road at the wrong time. Everybody know the two youth, know that they trouble nobody, grieve no human being. When Campbell Village people find out, they block the road with old car tires, and set the tires on fire.

It barely make the papers. "Two From Campbell Village Shot Dead", a skemps two-inch story on the bottom of a page so far into the newspaper that is only the big ad for "Tiger Condoms" right next door that make anybody notice it. Campbell Village people get in a worse rage. People call into Mr Jenkins' Talk Show. Some call Mrs Gladstone's show and some call Miss Compton-Riley. One big busload from the village go all the way to Kingston to Radio Jamaica to picket and make their complaint.

But none of it don't make no difference. Police Commissioner say they hold investigation and "the two young men were regrettably caught in the line of fire".

And that was that.

Ainsley see the parochial road to his right and he turn onto the rag-tag ribbon of marl and potholes with some stubborn strips of asphalt holding on here and there. When his thin-sole canvas shoes connect with the sharp point of the smallest stone, the stab pierce right up through his body like a injection needle.

Mama was right about Duarte, her "raise Cain" wash-belly. Time and again when Duarte is growing up, head-master bring complaints to Mama.

"Mistress Elder, I going to have to cane this boy if he keep on with this undisciplined behaviour. I don't like to cane, but Duarte not giving me no choice. He come to school and stay till recess time, then I can't find him nowhere in the afternoon. Or he don't come to school at all, even though I know that you have send him."

Always Mama say she will speak to Duarte about the bad behaviour and she is as good as her word. But it don't make one scrap of difference to him. She could save her breath.

"I going do better, Mama," he promise her. Then he do just what he choose.

At fourteen he stop school, say them not teaching him nothing. He say he playing football for Blackstars, which is the Campbell Village team. The local ganja don supply Blackstars with everything: boots, togs, vitamins, coach and equipment. Duarte say the coach tell him that he have talent and if he work hard, he can go to university in the USA on a football scholarship. Ainsley don't see how that could be, like how Duarte don't even finish school, but what he know?

Football is only one of Duarte's loves. The other one is Sharon, Sharon that Ainsley don't see this long time. When he not playing ball, Duarte forever gone over by Sharon, small quiet Sharon that sing in the choir at St Martin de Porres Church.

Duarte say he ask Sharon, "What kind of funny name that is for a church?"

Sharon say, "Cho, Duarte, you too foolish. St Martin is a black man."

"Seen," Duarte say. "That's why him is the poorest!"

Duarte take everything make fun and Sharon laughing all the time she with him. Duarte come to choir practice every Friday and Saturday evening and claim a pew in church to hear Sharon sing. When choir practice finish, he take time walk her home.

Ainsley is tired. His two feet moving only by instruction. The knife sticking him every now and then but is

no way he can run down the road with a knife in his hand
so better it stay in his pocket.

First time when Duarte just stop school, Ainsley find
some little things for him to do to earn a money. Ainsley
work with the Parish Council driving a truck. Any building or roadwork or bushing work have to come through
the Council Office at one time or another, so if there is
make-work, Ainsley get to know, and he arrange for
Duarte to earn couple coins to knock together in his
pocket.

All of a sudden one day, Ainsley hear Duarte
announce that he is going to Montego Bay to "hop a
charter" to Toronto. Ainsley don't know where Duarte
get passport and visa, where Duarte get money to buy
plane ticket, what business he have in foreign. But he
don't ask Duarte nothing. He is in fear of what he likely
to hear if he accost Duarte. Besides, he not able to take
on his baby brother for since Duarte turn man and move
gone to live in Puerto Bueno, he more stubborn than
ever. Ainsley don't have the strength nor the will to chal-
lenge him, even when one trip turn into two, and two
turn into three, and so they go on.

When he ready he tell himself that is the wildness in
Duarte that frighten him, the taint of the bad seed
which, never mind she try, Mama never manage to get

out of him. And after all, he, Ainsley, have his sick mother to think about. He pray and hope God Almighty will take Duarte's case.

Then this morning Ainsley get word at the Parish Council Office. A church-going friend of his who give classes to prisoners and hold services at the local jail leave a note with the security guard at the gate. He mark the note "URGENT".

"Duarte have a Glock and is not me one know. Stop him before he end up dead."

Ainsley panic. He can't figure out what Duarte need a gun for. His mind run on the don that bankroll Blackstars. Suppose the don and Duarte fight? Then he consider that maybe Duarte borrow money and can't pay it back. Maybe the moneylender send a gunman after Duarte and so Duarte carrying the Glock to defend himself. Maybe the reason Duarte is taking trips to Toronto is that he is transporting drugs, and maybe something go wrong with the deal.

He trying to think ahead and decide he going need a weapon so he take up a small kitchen knife. Miss Maisie, the office helper, proud of her knives that she sharpen with oil on a old-fashioned grindstone so, according to her, they stay sharp enough to take off a man head, if need be. He roll it in the washcloth he carry to mop up sweat and he stick it into his pants pocket.

If he want to find Duarte, the best person to check is Sharon. She don't live far, only thing the house is on top of a steep hill. When he hustling up the rise, he wonder if the reason that he don't see her this long time is that she and Duarte stop keeping company.

He reach exhausted, covered with sweat, panting like a dog.

"Then offer a man a glass of water nuh Miss Liza?"

This is how he greet Sharon's mother who is standing on the porch. Then he give out, "Where Sharon?"

Miss Liza's face furrow into a deep frown. She look at him up and down, and then turn to go inside. When Sharon appear, Ainsley's eyes nearly drop out of his head. Before him is a woman with a high belly, a full bosom resting on top of it. She is blowing her nose in a hanky, which she then crumple into a ball in her hand. On her fourth finger is a slim gold-coloured ring. He wonder who she think she is fooling.

"Where Duarte?"

Ainsley ask Sharon the question from the same place outside the house where he is standing.

Silence. Ainsley come up the steps.

"Me say, where is Du-ar-te?"

More silence.

Ainsley talk from back of clenched teeth.

"You hard of hearing? Me say where is Du-ar-te?"

"Don't know where Du-ar-te is."

Sharon's mimicking response fly up his nose, tunnel way up into the top of his head.

"You too damn lie."

Before Ainsley know what he is doing, he is back of her, his mouth to one ears, the knife slipped from the washrag in his pocket and up against her throat.

Sharon take time turn her head and look at him. Then she make a long kiss-teeth and say, "Gone down to the hotel."

"Look here gyal, don't provoke me. You expect me to search the whole big hotel? *Which part* of the hotel him gone?"

All of a sudden she change like a switch-colour lizard, spin to face him and shove the knife away from her neck.

"After I can't talk with that something into my neck. You want to know where he is? He take a gun and gone to find the don that stay at the hotel when month end come."

Miss Liza is standing in the doorway with a long glass of water. He don't stop to drink it. He know about that don. Everybody know about him for he not keeping himself secret. Letting it be known that he not like the Blackstars don that is just a little weed merchant. Letting it be known that he is a don gorgon, in charge of nuff small-time dons.

Ainsley looking to turn onto the main road now. So much sweat is running off his body that every stitch of clothes is soaking wet. He grab the knife out of his pants pocket for it looking to tear his trousers, and he suck his teeth and fling it far over into the bush on the roadside. What use is a so-so kitchen knife against a Glock?

The don that Duarte looking to tangle with do business in local and foreign. Ainsley don't even bother to remember stories about who get executed for what on his orders. What he do know, not as any story but as plain-as-day fact, is that in the early morning when the planes with weed, cocaine and heroin landing and taking off, police that have the hide-away airstrip under surveillance retire, for the don gorgon have enough troops and firepower on the runway to wage a small war.

Ainsley make a quick turn onto the main road. Is one main road into and out of Puerto Bueno, which is a tourist town, so all manner of transportation cruise it whole day and well into the night. He flag down a taxi. He is thinking hard about how Duarte come to have anything to do with the coke-and-heroin don. Duarte is a fool if he think he can take on that man.

When he see the crowd in front of Hotel Tropical, Ainsley's belly-bottom twist up. Not just a crowd. Plenty police. Four jeep, two police car, and a ambulance. Ainsley gorge rise, ready to jump out his mouth, for he sure Duarte dead.

"Jesus Christ." He talking out loud. "My mother mad. My one brother what left give woman pikni then get kill in a shootout. What me do to you, Massa God, to bring down this crosses?"

As the taxi pull over and stop and he jump out, he notice a body sprawl out in the open back of the biggest jeep. Two police stand up near it, one of them sporting a sub-machine gun. Never mind the distance, Ainsley can see that the short, thick man is not Duarte. In fact, the cargo of gold on his neck is plainly proclaiming that the dead man is the super don.

He start to push through the crowd towards the ambulance. The back doors still open and a medical looking fellow is talking to somebody on the ground. Ainsley send up a fervent prayer that the ambulance is there sake of Duarte for at least that would mean that he not dead. He make one almighty shove through five or six rows of people, leaving a wake of cursing as he break through, and he find himself in front of the ambulance rear doors and beside Inspector Harper, in charge of the Puerto Bueno Police Station and well-known to Ainsley, being as he was a senior student when Ainsley was a small boy at school.

"Is Duarte that in there, Supe?"

Harper nod.

"He in a bad way though, Ainsley."

Ainsley take a deep breath, using the inside part of his elbow to wipe sweat off his face, and ask, "I can go with him? If he so bad, he might dead before he reach hospital."

Harper rap at the now closing ambulance door and say, "Take this man, eh? Is the victim's brother."

Inside, Duarte lying on a stretcher-like bed with a tube in one arm and bandages across his whole front. His chest, as it lift and fall ever so slightly, make Ainsley think of a sleeping child. His face is relaxed, eyes closed. Except for the bloody bandages and the drip, Duarte could be taking sun on the beach.

As he come in and sit down, Duarte open his eyes. When he see Ainsley, he smile.

"Howdy, my brethren. I know you would come. I know you going take care of Sharon and the baby."

Then he close them again.

They ploughing through downtown Puerto Bueno. The blaring sirens don't do much to prod the marbling sludge of people who are crossing the road. Ainsley see two small boys, six or maybe seven years old, playing with crude machine guns carved out of wood. As the ambulance nudge and poke its way through shoppers and tourists, one small guerilla with a red kerchief across his forehead, peering out from behind a drum of garbage, sight the other one, take aim, and fire.

The one that is "shot" fling his weapon aside, grab his chest, twist, turn and wriggle in anguish until he drop onto the ground, "dead".

Ainsley don't dare take another look at Duarte's chest.

Limber Like Me...
For Betty

Limbo, limbo, limbo like me – limbo-o, limbo like me.

— Caribbean calypso

"Still limber, eh?" That is the Professor-man, greeting me.

Now, after three days of rain, emerald hills, and skies blue as the Virgin's frock. From the slope above the Falmouth campus, the church of Saint Francis romps with the sky, its cross catching at a wisp of cloud.

Should I try to tell this Professor-man about limberness? (Limberity? Or, maybe, limberacity?) Would he know it if it hit him in the eye? Or should I just rest-up-in-my-cosmic with the fact that the sight of my fat brown body clambering onto the campus over this barbwire fence can set his hormones humming? Still...

I smile at him. Wave. Take more time than I need to getting over the fence.

For the last four weeks of his life, my father sleep, wake, eat, speak to us with graduating effort, for a thin cauliflower necklace of cancer is slowly crocheting its way around his neck, and, same time, growing inward, blocking the tubes for air and food. Each day the floral pattern embellishes itself further, sprouting tiny new flowery facets.

Pops endure all these things with his head erect. Not stiff, mark you. Just sort of straight up, chin level with the ground and the bed. Is not a haughty head, just a head determined it not ready to flop forward or back, at any rate, not just yet. All the energy of him, brain that could tot up columns of figures faster than fingers could put them into a calculator, hands that delight to draw 'plans' for houses, dresses for our paper dolls, the occasional sketch of a hibiscus or a hurricane-felled tree; arms that could saw and chisel and carve and summon cabinets and tables from a log of lignum vitae—all this purpose, this will, focused in that rock steady head.

It was an extraordinary feat, and I only recognize it near to his dying. I only realize what he *mean* the head to do, and that it doing what he mean it to, the night before the morning that he die.

Pops' dying hit Ricardo the hardest. He was Pops' best friend, and Pops was his other self. They had bank accounts in common and knew about each other's women when Carmencita and I still thought most men were faithful to their wives. Now we all sitting on Carmencita's verandah, gazing out at the sea, our lives' business put one-side for the minute.

The afternoon is lit by a gold tongue of flame at the throat of the green lizard inhabiting the coolest corner of the verandah. We are smart and perceive the brilliant obtrusion as trumpery and deceit, since the lizard don't use that tongue to eat, only to lure his unsuspecting dinner.

We work with Pops all the way through his dying, but it was a thing he *did*. He never suffer it, or permit it to happen, or give in to it. He set his life aside, determined it. His dying was a thing he shaped and moulded, as he had done things all his life, without ceremony but with great care. By the time he had decided he had best complete his dying, he wasn't afraid anymore.

Is just as well sickness give people a lot of things to do. Turn on the oxygen. Turn it off. Wheel it in. Open it with a wrench. Lock it up. Misplace the wrench. Find it back. Bathe the sick one. Invent ways to wash the hair on the head of a prone somebody without drowning him. Brush the said hair. Brush it again. Put up brush and comb. Take them out again to repeat the ritual not half an hour later. Care the patient in a thousand small-small ways...

I arrange that the Professor-man keep a ways ahead of me on one of the myriad tracks of hard-packed earth that lazy, bad-minded, own-way students on this university campus have carved across the green grass—poor grass, struggling to survive with not a help from anything or anybody except the seasonal rain. I say 'a ways ahead' for in my creole way, fifty feet, fifty yards, fifty metres, is the same thing.

Miles, I know, is longer.

One time me and El Professor were friends. Not sleeping friends. Friend-friends. One day when I was slim and beautiful—"tan bella," he'd say, winking appreciatively—we had gone together into Queenstown to hear Derek Walcott read at the Little Theatre. Well, we never really go *together.* (He have wife: a tall, thin, shrill, jealous black package. I have husband: shortish, whitish, secure and indulgent.) I need a ride. He say "So, come with me." I go.

It was hot. Little Theatre still appealing for funds to install central air. On the way back, he stop his new Toyota on the southwest corner of the Racecourse and buy us sno-cone from a one-hand sno-cone man—well, not really a man. More a boy. The Professor-man ask him about the arm and he shrug.

"Is accident. When me small, me bredda push me and me drop pon de power saw and it cut off." He laughs wryly. "No hospital not in my part of South."

South is the south of the island. It is, to South people, a special, separate country.

His one hand more than make up for the missing second one.

So my sno-cone done and all my little bits and pieces

dripping with the last of the passion fruit syrup. The Professor-man offers a handkerchief and I wipe my fingers and my mouth, and give it back to him. Guess what? The man no gimme back the hanky! I feel like a little messy girl, my messiness summarily returned to my own safekeeping. When I come back from the slap, having kept my head lowered to stuff the hanky into my bag, I purse my mouth like I smell something bad.

El Professor: "Something the matter?"

I too vex. But I only say, "Nothing worth worrying about."

And then I smile, for I picturing what is like to make love to this man. And I smile broader, for I relishing the shortish whitish man I screwing these many years, and grinning at the toilet paper joke we share so many times when, wet with each other, rank as goats, we tumble over into sleep.

Near to the end, when Pops finding it hard to speak, he issue a new summons. We never know what he was saying at first, but after he say it to Carmencita, me, Nurse Howden, we finally make it out.

"Nurse me."

So we croon to him. Hold his hand. Pat his arms. Mop sweat from his forehead. Kiss it. Powder him. Put ointment on the jewel at his throat. Anoint it again and again. Put over-proof white rum on his head. Hold the rum bottle to his nose so he can suck the smell in. Examine his feet for swelling. Talk to them. Talk to his lungs. Encourage the working parts to co-operate, secure the body, patient, wounded on the bed.

And Pops lie down in it like a baby and let it suckle him, this man that brew reseda and comfrey for ailments of man and beast, that know the virtues of periwinkle bush before the modern medical researchers find them out, that slap together and apply a poultice like any medicine man.

Ricardo and Pops and Roderick (my short nasty man) have one drink of ponche crema every day up to the last Sunday Pops live. He die early the third Monday morning after Christmas. At least, Ricardo and Roderick drink. Pops take small sips of the white liquour and let it lie at the back of his throat. Sometimes, near the end, an hour or two after the drinking is done, he would cough, and the creamy liquid would run from the sides of his mouth, and we would know that not a drop had got past the bung at his throat.

The night before that Monday morning, it dawn on me that for as long as Pops head hold up straight, he not going to die. Simple as that. It was his way of checking on his presence, of ensuring his being here. Suddenly I know that his head wouldn't go down till he decide he going. When pillow receive head, Pops fixing to move on.

So Ricardo and me and Carmencita gazing at the sea, fussing about what we going to do about Pops. Never mind how we mince-up the food, purée the food, liquefy it in a blender, not a thing going past Pops' throat. Pops eat and hold the mush in his throat for hours, determined he still in control, resolved not to give trouble.

(Well, not in everything, for while he still had his voice, when we were droning the rosary, muttering our "Holy Mary, Mother of God, pray for us sinners now and at the hour of our death" with grim monotony, when he can take no more of this reiterated woefulness, he terminate the exercise with a roar of "Basta!" and we scatter, frightened just like when we small.)

We know this is not a man you feed through a tube. True, he ask to be nursed, but equally true he resent his lack of control over his bowels and his bladder. He long for the freedom to shave his own chin and bathe his own body and ablute at length on the throne of his house, peering through his glasses, newspaper on his knees.

Ensconced in his own home, imperial on that throne, he has done the crossword, the whole London cryptic puzzle, in no more than ten minutes, every day of his life. He had constructed the throne room and installed the throne in that house with his very own hands; had added extra bedrooms to the modest structure, as his family increased;

arranged front and back verandahs; redone the kitchen in modern style. With his hands he had raised uprights, mixed cement and sand and stone to make concrete nog walls; rendered them, painted them, hurricane-strapped the roof to cheat the rains and storms.

This is not a man you feed through a tube.

As I near the Social Sciences block, the Professor-man is ascending the stairs, two at a time. I will go up the stairs too and pass his office en route to the department office. (I am a post-grad student doing my PhD.) I avoid catching up, don't stick my head into his office as I go by.

One day not long after we had gone to hear Walcott read I had stopped to collect a paper that he had graded—"Gender as an Economic Variable: the Case of Antigua, a Small Island-state"—and he had proffered a poem. Roderick the Nasty is a poet so I have for many years had an intelligent interest. "On Angels and Pinheads", he had called it.

I recognized the metaphysical riddle in the title for they sent me to Catholic college in the USA, the good nuns who raised me. We are an old Cuban family, moved to the island in the nineteenth century, wombed in the church. The nuns were not about to lose me to a secular institution like the new University here, not, at any rate, until I had been inoculated with Ethics, Moral Theology,

and the generous helpings of Thomas Aquinas's *Summa*,
compulsory at every Catholic college.
I read:

On Angels and Pinheads

If an angel alight
at the side of its twin,
does that narrow the room
on the head of the pin?

As the angels keep landing
and taxiing in,
does the temperature rise
on the tip of that pin?

Is docility, virtue?
Agility, sin?
Do they only do dancing
aloft on the pin?

I imagine them seraphs
must be pretty packed in,
as they make terpsichorean
twirling out, twisting in.

If I were an angel
(which I've never been),

I'd sure wish you a-lit
on the head of my pin!

I thought, "Is this what the psychology folks mean by passive-aggressive?" But I kept that to myself, as I smiled and returned it to him. "Clever, clever," I said. "You clearly have a livelihood there."

Then I thought of the passion-fruit-stained handkerchief, and my nasty Roderick, and my father who had wooed my mother with sonnets which he wrote himself and gave to her on the tenth of every month, the anniversary of the day he met her. And I smiled again. My farewell.

"Listen to me, you Miss Angela!" Carmencita was bearing down on me, her ackee-seed eyes wide, her small mouth stretched so you couldn't see any lips, "this is not your house. My father, your father, our father, is a sick in my house. Not yours. When anything happen and we can't manage it, and Pops suffer or die as a result, is my conscience it going burden and is me going to feel bad. Him cyaan't stay here no longer. We cyaan't manage him."

So the last petals of cauliflower find their way into the decoration around my father's neck.

"Pops," I say to him, "you must be really tired."

He smile a weak smile. Then, his eyes make four with mine and his head drop back onto the pillow.

"True," he say with surprising clarity. "I feel a little weary. I going retire early tonight."

Nurse Howden say he slept off lightly, without even a gasp of breath, at about five the next morning. Carmencita say, as usual, he resolve our differences. Me, I affirm the maker's energy in my father's head erect, the appreciation of simple kindnesses, the savouring of the streamlined functions of a sane body.

So today I am on campus again, to explain my absence from tutorials and ask for grace on my next paper, for we must bury Pops and I know I won't make the due-date. The Professor-man has gone into his room and closed the door, and it is quiet as I walk past, so I decide that he is busy and that I will leave him a note.

"My father died this morning," I write, "so things will be busy and confused over the next two weeks or so. I'm hoping it will be all right to give in my paper, due in three days' time, at the end of the month. If I can't have the benefit of so long an extension, please let me know what you propose. Thanks. Blessings. Angela."

I think about the "Blessings", for the Professor-man isn't into God and all that stuff, but my father has just died, and I decide to damn well let them stay.

I slip the note into an envelope and hand it to Sita Ramlal. She knows Pops well and knows that he has gone; she will make roti and curry for after the funeral. Sita is sixty plus, East Indian, and guards the Professor-man's secrets. She is a loyal secretary but a good woman too.

On my way out of her office, I execute a perfect backbend. This is a bit of craziness I indulge in sometimes, to Sita's great amusement. We aren't bosom buddies, but we are big women together in many things. We share babysitting (my children, her grandchildren), broken diets, broken promises, and also uproarious jokes including, defensively, a collection concerning positions in the Kamasutra and the talent of experienced bones, when the brashly bared bodies of the undergrads and their manners manqué start to get to us.

No one has 'caught' me doing my backbends up to now.

Sita thinks I am crazy.

"Yeah, yeah. You're still agile—and an ass! Your father," she smiles wider and wider, "must be doing the limbo in his grave!"

I kiss her on the forehead.

"From Pops," I say. "He is going to miss your curry."

The Game

Clouds trotted towards the mountains. It was like that in the mornings. In the early afternoon, they would burst into rain, heavy hard downpours of thick drops that would be gone as quickly as they had come.

"Aggression is just if it's directed against persons who are evil."

"In that case, we should be shooting every merchant in this city."

The two men laughed. They were sitting at a table on the pavement. It was hot. They lifted their bare forearms to wipe sweat from their brows as if moving one hand. A breeze was already starting to blow up from the sea, the same one that had cooled their ancestors, *conversos* sailing into the harbour with Columbus in the first ships on their way from Spain.

The older one, somewhere between thirty and fifty, signaled a passing waiter to bring them more coffee.

"You know you shouldn't have a second cup. You're forgetting you're all hypertensive. The doctor said one."

The younger one, no more than nineteen and as like the older one as a smaller pea in a greener pod, shook an accusatory finger.

"Doctor, schmockter. Something has to kill me, kill you, kill us all."

On the street, three children, stepped up in size like an illustration for a grammar book, were playing with a stone. It was a made-up game. The bat was the thick stem of a coconut palm frond, wielded like a baseball bat. The ball was a stone, bowled rather than pitched toward a bit of cardboard, a wicket anchored ingeniously between three largish rocks.

"You would fight then, if they drafted you?"

"Without question."

"What if they sent you to kill your cousins, your friends?"

"Why should they do that?"

"The King of England that abdicated, you know, the one that married the wealthy American woman..."

"I know the one."

"He supported the Germans. He liked Hitler. They don't make much of it in the history books, but it was so."

"Well, his children, had he had any, might have been obliged to aim guns at their cousins. I don't exactly think it's likely in our situation."

"Ah, but they are our cousins, passionate warriors, just as we are. Convinced, like us, that God is on their side."

"They've taught you young ones badly. You see too many sides. You need to have a point of view."

There was a shriek of delight from the street as the stone thwacked the cardboard and the batter threw aside his bat, disgusted with himself. The shortest one, a rather round but nonetheless agile fielder, ran forward to capture the stone. The tallest, the batsman, adjusting the brim of a baseball cap that announced that he (presumably) was "Ahmed", sulked good-naturedly off to the side. The bowler took the bat.

"I don't like war. Any war. I think war is evil."

"I don't think your opinion counts. War is as old as the race, as old as Cain killing Abel. We're not talking about whether or not to fight. We're talking about when it's *right*—or wrong."

The waiter brought them more coffee. They paused while he poured.

"I am saying that it is never right to fight. I am saying that there are ways to solve disagreements that do not involve murder."

"Ariel must mean ethereal. You've told this to your mother?"

"My mother is a bloodthirsty hussy."

"Well, that's something we can agree on, anyway."

They leaned back in their chairs, away from the aroma of the coffee, and laughed again.

There was another shout from the street, and the bowler ran forward.

"My time to bat, Ali! My time, my time."

They turned towards the game. The bat was as tall as

the new batsman. Ali, heading out into the field, said, "You need to stand in front of the cardboard, Joshua. Otherwise, there's no point."

The breeze from the sea had picked up. Across the street the traders were throwing up their shutters. A young man, serious and oddly thick about the middle, stepped up the stairs into the café.

Ahmed bowled.

Rocks of every size rained down.

Shining Waters

"I don't mean to talk out of turn, reverend father, but I saying again that it's not right for a man of God to go out into the street looking so."

If Constantia felt no diffidence about speaking her mind to the priest, it was on account of Amy Forde, she that used to be housekeeper in the rectory at Shining Waters before Constantia took on the job. She had been 'prenticed' to Miss Amy, so the work fell to her when Miss Amy's big-woman self dropped down dead from a heart attack one Friday in Lent as she was cooking ackee and codfish in the breezy outside shed of a kitchen.

For twenty-three years Miss Amy had run the rectory at St John of the Cross. She had insisted that it was 'the fathers' home', inventing both a name and language for the place. The priests were 'reverend father'. Reverend fathers did not get up and go to bed; they arose and retired; they were absent, not gone out, indisposed, not sick, unavailable, not busy.

Miss Amy had also prescribed ways for administering the 'home', rites related to washing and ironing, cooking and cleaning, baking and shopping for the household.

Ritual made for Orderliness, which was next to Cleanliness, which was next to Godliness.

Constantia had been a faithful disciple, preserving everything of Miss Amy's language and culture, and it was out of this history and heritage that she spoke firmly to the young man before her. He was standing in the door of her kitchen soaked to his see-through blue-white skin looking out into a drubbing rain.

"Miss C," the words came over his shoulder, his back turned so water spilling from the white T-shirt he was wringing out landed on the stained-red concrete steps, not in the kitchen, "it's just a walk that I take and a-went down to the shop to buy the smokes." He indicated the pack of cigarettes on the table. "No somebody in the Mothers' Union did never see me."

They hadn't wanted a Mothers' Union because Mothers' Unions were Anglican, not Catholic. What wasn't Catholic? Mothers? A Union? The hat and gloves tea ladies of the Catholic Women's League gave him the heebie-jeebies, so St John's had a Mothers' Union.

Constantia sneezed.

"Bless you."

She blew her nose, looked through the window at the downpour that had at least held up long enough to allow her to reach the fathers' home at just past twelve o'clock. It was slapping walls and roofs upside their heads like they were bad-behaved children. She wished she could slap him just so. She'd no idea how it was going to work out between them. His smoking irritated her. His attempts at talking local irritated her. His refusal to dress himself in a manner suited to someone of his status irritated her. In all her time in the father's home, there had been no priest, young or old, like this one.

"In any case, reverend father," Constantia honked into her handkerchief, "you will please to change the wet clothes."

A death rattle on the roof of the rectory and lightning prancing through the small kitchen whenever it felt like, thunder roiling in its wake. Inside his bedroom, Mère, the dog, had taken refuge under the bed. Not that Martin didn't thank God for rain on this day, clouds low and close, their sooty bellies threatening to disgorge something vile. His mental state was doubtless what made him see the weather so, but so what? It was all perception anyhow, the world itself being only What-God-Saw. Maybe God should change his glasses.

Racing up the hill from the corner just now, ten-pack of cigarettes under his shirt, he'd been relieved to feel the cool drops, know it was plain rain. He lit a cigarette, picked up the cracked cup he used as an ashtray, went into his little mousehole of a study.

He could hear Constantia.

"I don't think smoking is a sin you know reverend

father, not in a world where people raping, bombing and murdering every day. But is not good for the human body, so kindly please don't do it in my vicinity."

Having been careful to wring the excess water out at the door of the kitchen, he dragged the damp T-shirt over his head and flung it onto the ground, pulled out the straight-backed wooden chair and took a seat at the mahogany desk, remembering another of Constantia's cautions: "That desk worth more than this whole house, reverend father, so please treat accordingly."

As far as he could determine, Constantia saw no contra-diction whatsoever in calling him reverend father on one hand and treating him like a wayward child on the other. He wasn't sure she liked him, but then a lot of people did-n't like him. He sucked on the cigarette, blew out three per-fect circles. He loved blowing smoke circles, a skill he'd honed whiling away innumerable absences from school.

The rings floated into Constantia's face, which appeared round the door.

"Thank-you-please for the wet shirt, reverend father," she pointed to it on the floor, "and the trousers, a little from now as you are able."

She snuffled. He made no apology for his nakedness. After all, she hadn't knocked. It wasn't his fault that the study had no door.

"And just to make you know that the boy, Calvin, come round here when you was absent down the road. Pardon my not remembering to tell you straight away as soon as you came in."

Constantia's capacity for using completely correct English structures, placing them seamlessly into her island talk, still amazed him. Or maybe she blanket-stitched island talk into the English—it was equally impressive.

"Did he say what he wanted, Miss C?"

"Father, you know full well I not taking no message from the likes of that boy. He only say to tell you that he come. Look like he just see a duppy, all the same."

"He's a child of God, you know Miss C, heir of the kingdom, like you and me."

She fixed her hands akimbo, looked at him unbelieving, shrugged elaborately, and walked off.

Well, more like me, Martin Rouzaud thought. He wondered why Calvin hadn't stayed. The trip to the shop hadn't taken very long, so he must have been in a hurry.

Deserting the mousehole, he took his trousers off in the bathroom and on the way into the bedroom, deposited them in the clothesbasket in the hallway. His life had come full circle. His mother had hand-washed his clothes till he took the bus to the seminary at age nineteen. Now another woman did for him in the same way, one as tall, tough, and forthright as his mother, and one that didn't like him, as he suspected his mother had not done either.

Which was okay. Affection ebbed and flowed, its movement unredeemed by the dependability of the tide. Goodwill had collapsed without warning in his life, so he didn't trust it: no friends at school, no friends at the seminary either. When he'd come in late and smelly from the long walks that kept him sane, his fellow seminarians sniffed their displeasure as they passed him. It was absurd: What kind of brotherhood depended on deodorant and a daily shower?

It was more important that his mother had respected him, understood that her loutish son was the stub-of-the-toe that proved the world existed. Bishop Berkeley and Dr Johnson, wasn't it? If you don't believe there's a world out there, wait till you stub your toe? He thought Constantia took him seriously as well. And he liked her, as he had liked his mother, for they weren't women to be trifled with. Like God, they had dominion.

He sat on the bed, exhausted. He'd spent yesterday morning trying to figure out ways of establishing a little dominion too, and the afternoon driving to High Village to talk to his boss about his thoughts.

Jim Watson, the Order's superior, ran a co-op in High Village. It was a centre for a whole set of cottage industries: pineapples, guavas and citrus fruit were the ingredients in sweets, preserves and jellies; various kinds of palm and thatch produced brooms, mats, hats and handbags; there was even a health drink brewed from roots and mosses. The products were branded, HighvilPro. With some professional help in packaging and marketing, they were doing very well.

So he seemed a good person to talk to.

"The land is there, Jim. Deeded in 1927 to the town of Shining Waters by some eccentric wealthy planter-type named Montague. There was something about the government annexing it at one point for the purpose of building a road, but if there were such a plan, it's long since been shelved. A hundred acres of prime agricultural land, doing nothing."

"*You* think it's doing nothing."

"It's obvious that it's doing nothing."

"Nothing in this island is obvious, least of all what's being cultivated on prime agricultural land."

"You mean there's a ganja plantation in there, with an airstrip and a garrison of armed guards?"

"I don't know. But there may be. There could be a homegrown small-munitions factory, or a lab for processing coke. There could be another Consulate, for all I know."

Martin knew about Consulate. It was a district off the old Mine Road in the Patridge Mountains where anyone with enough money could get a passport or visa for anywhere in the world. The documents usually took a week, rarely more than two. But that was his whole point. There was more ingenuity, talent, skill, and sheer energy in the place than anywhere else he'd been or knew of. He wanted to get permission from whoever was the rightful person so the youth in Shining—they called it that, or 'Waters'—could use the land, grow vegetables for the hotels or the residential college nearby. Or maybe the business people in the area would sponsor a school so they could learn trades and crafts, carpentry, mechanics, carving, painting, how to play a musical instrument, anything to make a living.

The superior said he should soft-pedal it.

"Have you told anybody about this?"

"Only Calvin. He's a youngster who's been helping me work on the shed in back."

"Has he told anyone?"

"I don't know. He could have told his friend Lucky. He could have told anybody. I wasn't broadcasting what I was thinking about the land but I wasn't exactly treating it as a secret."

"Well, I wouldn't talk about it just yet."

"Come to think of it, didn't you have a bit of trouble setting up the centre that you have up here?"

"It was more than 'a bit of trouble', Martin. It pretty near got me whacked. And I'm not certain we're over with it yet, which is precisely why I think you should go forward carefully. Let me do some checking around and call you in a couple of days."

They'd talked for a bit more, eaten some fried fish and bammy and then Jim waved him off.

"And don't pick up anybody on your way down this mountainside either," he'd said as he slapped the back of the 1975 VW bug. "Coward man keep safe bone."

Well, he wasn't a coward man.

He made good time down the hill, stopping at the

corner of Aqua Vale Road and the main coast road at about six. As he waited to cross to the left side of the road—he still wasn't accustomed to that—and head east towards Shining, he looked the other way and was blinded by a perfect apple of sun, magnificently bloodied by pollution.

"Don't turn yu head. If you see me, yu dead."

How and when the man had got into the car, Martin couldn't think. Maybe what he'd imagined as a split-second glance at the bleeding sun had in fact been a transfixed stare, but he doubted that. Maybe the roar of trucks on the highway had masked the noise of the door opening and closing. The man must have moved quick as a dervish. Whatever the explanation, the muzzle of a gun was pressing into his ribs.

"Drive. Me wi tell yu whe fe go. Just look pon de road. Seen?"

Martin nodded, not trusting himself to speak. He gripped the wheel and pressed the gas pedal, controlling an impulse to twist the car off the road and ram it into a light pole, a wall, even an oncoming vehicle.

"Keep pon dis road. When me tell yu, yu gwine mek a sharp turn left an go dung a cliffside. Just tek time drive ordinary-like."

Out of the farthest corner of his eye, he got a hint of his companion: shorter than he was, and thick. His voice said so. Too, he had a sense of big-man bulk filling the Bug, and a feeling of ample weight in the next seat.

Ten minutes later, the light having turned honey, purple, then pale pink, the voice spoke again.

"See de big tree yonder on de bankside? Look good yu see a turn off in front dere. Take it. Slow and easy, for de road drop straight down."

The little car, assisted by the heavy passenger, held the steep road like a goat. At the bottom of the hill was a flat area of solid limestone worn smooth by waves, and in front of it, an arc of white sand cupping a miniscule bay.

"Get out. Lef de key inna de cyaar. So far yu smart. Gun still a-watch yu so no bodda make no funny move. And gwaan keep yu yeye to yuself."

Martin did as he was told. He was cold with fury now, but he'd no doubt the man would kill him if he tried anything. Looking out to sea, he saw a small rowboat, the kind local fishermen used, pulling in. It was just far enough away not to see what was happening, and he was glad.

"Yu smart, yes. Maybe it save yu life." The car sighed giving up the man's weight. "Me doan decide yet. Gwaan go lie down put yu face in de sand, foot up yaso, head out dehso."

Martin stretched out, his feet touching the cliff wall, his head almost into water that gathered round his torso as it settled into the sand at the sea's edge. He rested his head on his forearms, facing away from the man.

"Stay deh till de fisherman-dem reach. Dat time yu cyan get up. And no bodda tell Babylon for me know whey yu live. Yu shoulda gi Jesus tanx me doan blood yu tidday."

He listened as the man settled back into the car and the door slammed. Gears engaged—reverse, forward, reverse again—then he heard the Bug fighting its way up the hill.

He lay there till the sound of the car had ceased completely. When he rose, the fishermen were waving at him. He returned the wave but didn't wait for them to reach the beach. What was the point? Their lives were hard enough already. He took off his wet shoes, went swiftly up the slippery hillside and put the shoes back on, deciding to walk till he saw a taxi. The man hadn't wanted money, just the car. He had dollars enough to get home.

"Reverend father, I going now. I asking you please to come and throw the deadbolts on this door."

She spoke as she gathered up her handbag, the shutpan with her dinner, her umbrella, the newspaper, and her reading glasses. She knew that the priest wasn't going to come and shut the door, but it was up to her to remind him, so she did. Shining wasn't a safe quiet country town any more.

When the priest had sent her home early on account of the sniffling, she hadn't objected. She felt tired, her throat was sore, and stuff was gathering on her chest. Picking her way on the sodden track that went from the rectory down past the shop where the priest bought his smokes, she rejoiced as she always did in the after-rain countryside. It reminded her of a just-bathed baby, cool and clean and dripping, waiting for the sun to pat it dry.

She reached into her pocket for her kerchief to blow her nose. That was another thing. This reverend father refused to use handkerchiefs and was walking around with a washrag, wiping his face with it. She wondered what company he was keeping for him to come to that pass. A washrag!

It bothered her that this reverend spent more time outside of the rectory than any of the other priests she had worked for. It was not that she thought he went to any places where he oughtn't to go, but his continued absences were unsettling. When she had raised the matter delicately, as Miss Amy would have wished, and asked whether she might help take care of some of the things he was doing out on the road, he'd said thank you but he could manage.

"I'm just learning about the parish, Miss C. A good shepherd has to know his flock. Jesus didn't cool his heels in an office in Nazareth, don't it?"

She didn't bother carry him nor bring him on that one. She felt sure the Almighty would back her concerning the clothes, though. The first time she saw him go out in washed-out jeans and a flimsy white undershirt, she had controlled her tongue. Next day, she had said her say. He took a while before he answered.

"Look, Miss C. I've worn clothes like this all my life.

They suit me. I feel comfortable in them. I didn't give up wearing them when I was in the seminary, and they upset a lot of people then. Truth is, I find that they don't disturb most folks. And they don't stop me from doing my job."

Shortly after that he had started going outside in the yard and working without his shoes, and then walking out into the road barefooted. Sometimes in the week he even said Mass with no shoes on. She thought maybe it was to provoke her, but since he didn't really bother her much, just let her carry on with what she had to do, she figured he was just suiting himself, like he said.

People did notice it. Some said it was not nice but most said, "No big ting." After all, plenty white tourists never wore any shoes. And there were some people who were very loud in their support.

"After it don't hold him back. Him manage to find a next nurse so clinic can open every day now, so him could walk on him hand for all I care."

The young miss who said that was in Constantia's opinion quite common but the remark made her smile all the same. She was still smiling when she elbowed her way into the minibus a while later.

"Reverend father, I going now." He heard the stuff on her chest thickening Constantia's voice. "I asking you please to come and throw the deadbolts on this door."

He didn't know when he had fallen back on the bed. The noises Constantia made lapping to and fro about last minute things continued faintly. He heard her go through the door, calling behind her, "Have a God-bless evening, reverend father, till tomorrow. I feed the dog. She look like she soon drop the puppies." There were people waiting for those puppies. Mère was a good watch.

"Goodnight, Miss C," he pretended to shout, knowing that she would not expect to hear him.

Last night when he'd finally got to the rectory, having walked far before he'd got a taxi ride, it had been well after nine. She had left dinner, escoveitched fish and yellow yam. It was tart, zingy, as he liked it. He used his fingers, poking it down his throat, at the same time trying to call Jim Watson's residence. The calls would not go through and the phone kept slipping from his greasy fingers. He'd tried the HighvilPro office too, with no luck.

The Waters police station was on the other side of town, and he hadn't been able to decide whether to go there or even try phoning, not because of the thief's warning but because he wanted to talk to Jim Watson first. Besides, if he'd gone to the station, what could he have reported? That someone whom he had not seen and could therefore not describe had abducted him at gunpoint? The car he would in time report stolen, though he was sure it would be abandoned, once it had served the man's purpose. He'd get it back eventually.

The forces that must have shaped his abductor preoccupied him. The man had counseled that he should thank Jesus for his life—a murderer counseling a priest to give thanks to God! The place was amazing. The bishop had said one of its problems was there were too many self-made men. "They make themselves, and do a lousy job." But according to what were they supposed to make themselves? Where was a person supposed to get an idea of self, a pattern to follow as they put brick upon brick? Parents? Teachers? Politicians? Preachers?

There was the fall day that his mother learned of his life plan.

"Priest?" She had been incredulous. "You, my only boy child, which I've raised one-handed, and you're saying you want to be a priest?

"God, Mom. God wants it."

"God wants you to be a priest?"

"Yes he does. I'm sure of it."

"Sure you're sure. 'Sure' will be the death of you."

He'd slept and woken abruptly to see Calvin, barefoot and unkempt, gazing at him through his open bedroom door, one arm holding his side, blood oozing onto his shirt from the spot at his waist that he was supporting. He leapt from the bed blinking his eyes to clear away sleep, and found he was quite alone.

The dream of Calvin didn't unnerve him. He'd been

an orderly in the hospital in his ramshackle hometown. Once a small but bustling port on Lake Ontario, it had become a ghost town when the trains that hauled goods in and out were re-routed. It wasn't long till it became down-at-heel quarters for an agglomeration of households headed by out-of-work men, good Irish Catholics who made babies on their wives each year, never mind the absence of a means to feed them. Anger erupted often enough there, so he was no stranger to the work of a fierce person with a weapon.

But what he knew about Calvin did not include any history of violence, so he had no idea what would have occasioned such a dream. Not that he really knew much about the youth. They had met on another rainy day when his VW had, contrary to legend, stalled. Bogged down in an enormous pothole, he had been glad when Calvin and his friend, Lucky, pushed him out.

The two had been waiting for a bus on the outskirts of Waters at the corner of the main road and the secondary road that led up to Laughlands. In fact, the encounter with Calvin and Lucky had confirmed in his mind the project he'd been hatching with the empty land.

"So you going to be on time for work?" he'd asked as they drove alongside the sour gray sea, for after their Good Samaritan deed, he'd offered them a lift into town. The storm clouds, their business done, were drifting towards the horizon.

"No work for youth in these parts, parson," Calvin

spoke for the two of them.

"So what takes you into town then?"

The young men looked at each other.

"Man that live in Hope not going to die in Gutters."
This came from Lucky, accompanied by laughter from
them both.

"Well, maybe you can pass by the rectory and cut the
grass or give a hand with repairs sometime. I can't pay
much but I'd be glad for the help."

It was all he could think of to say as they clambered out
of the small car, leaping over the trench of brown soupy
water in which the morning's detritus of plastic bags, pop
cans and a bright aquamarine condom floated. Another
eight-or-so chaps of their age stood on the corner.

Monday morning of the following week, Calvin had
arrived at the rectory, mopping up the sweat that the
long road up the hill had drawn with a washrag that he
pulled from the pocket of his jeans. He had been outside
in the yard working on the shed, a collapsing structure
that had once been the rectory kitchen, so the youngster
was spared the security guard treatment that Constantia
meted out to strangers.

"Morning, parson."

"Howdy, Calvin. Glad to see you. How are things?"

Calvin got to the point.

"You say I could come and help out, so I come. I
bring my work clothes." He pointed to the bag on his
shoulder.

"Right. Fine. You can help me with this." He pointed to the shed.

"Don't think anybody can help you with that, parson," Calvin laughed.

"Laugh if you like, but I intend to make this into a good sturdy structure, so you'd better make up your mind whether you are on the job or not."

He stood straight up as he spoke, unfolding taller than most people expected. He saw Calvin's eyes measure him, saw them drop to his bare feet. Lifting the pickaxe that was leaning against one corner of the shed, he spun it into the air and brought it down hard into a cracked chunk of concrete that had been supporting a corner upright.

"We need to shore this up." He spoke as he worked. "I've propped up the roof. So we dig this concrete out, put in a new foundation, and a new post. We start here, do each corner in turn."

He loosened the pickaxe from the splintered concrete, looked up at the youth and saw that he'd made up his mind.

"How much you pay for a day's work?"

"How much you charge?"

They'd worked on the shed for five days in all, putting up the supports, reframing and re-anchoring the roof. Then the rains had begun in earnest. He'd had to send Calvin home more than once because the sky just wouldn't stay closed.

It didn't take him long to put to rest the spectre of the bleeding youth. He prayed about it and then gave it to God. He'd been still tired, wanting to go back to sleep. Curious about how far the night had gone, he got up and looked outside. The sky was deep black. It was nowhere close to morning. He'd fallen back on the pillows and into another deep sleep, waking only when Constantia arrived, later than usual because it was Friday and she would have been to market. Roused by her noises in the kitchen, alarmed by the time and dying for a cigarette, he'd gotten up, dragged on his clothes and headed down the road to the shop.

Constantia closed her eyes. She usually managed a nap between Shining and Rio Largo. Her body knew how long it took; it would wake her just in time for her to shout out, "One stop, driver," so he'd know to let her off.

This evening she couldn't sleep though, and for no good reason. Maybe she was worried about the dog. The bitch's belly was enormous, so the litter would probably be seven or eight. There were lots of people wanting the puppies for Mère was beautiful, a rusty red dog with a thick coat and a tail like one of those feathers that stuck out of Marcus Garvey's hat. She was feeling that she should be there for when the puppies were coming. What if the mother dog was to eat all the puppies? That happened sometimes and she couldn't bear the thought of it. Then she rebuked herself for her own foolishness. What she should have been worrying about was the whole heap of trouble that the pups were going to be, the extra work she would have until their owners came to collect them.

Truth to tell she knew full well what was bothering her. It was the fellow Calvin. She didn't like him, neither the look nor the smell of him, didn't trust the designer jeans and the expensive essence. True he did the work, and he talked respectfully, but from the first day she saw him her spirit never took to him. The afternoon of the second day when she left a little after him, she saw him heading up the hill instead of down the road to town. Nothing was supposed to be up that hill, just bush. But for months now people in Waters were whispering about a farm up there that was growing ganja in some newfangled way and, more than that, cultivating some other plant that nobody had ever seen before.

So what could Calvin be doing striding up that track, walking as if he have business going to?

They were passing by Lessings when her eye caught it, and she realized that she had not seen it at the father's home during the day, the blue VW Bug in a ditch on the side of the road.

"It's me, Jim. Martin."

"Hello? Who? Oh! Martin! Thank God. Are you okay?"

"I'm fine. I've been trying to get you since last night."

"Listen," there was trepidation in the voice, "I'm just relieved to hear from you. The police in Lessings called a couple hours ago to say they'd found your VW in a ditch beside the main road. It's registered to the Society so they called me. I've been phoning you since then but not getting through. I guess maybe because of the rain. Thank God you're okay. What in Christ's name happened?"

"Well, seems I survived an encounter with an armed villain on my way back to Shining Waters yesterday."

"You *what?*"

"I was briefly abducted on my way back from your homestead. I'm waiting at the Aqua Vale corner, about to turn onto the main road, and in jumps this guy and jams a gun into my ribs."

"You're joking!"

"Never been more serious in my life."

"So what did you do?"

"He was considerate enough, told me not to look at him or I'd be dead, instructed me to drive where he directed me, which I did."

"Martin, you're sounding very cavalier about this. It's not something to be made light of."

"Believe me, Jim, I'm glad to be here to make light, heavy, or anything else of it. To be honest, I was so angry

I had a difficult time stopping myself from doing something rash."

"Aha! That famous temper! I thought they sent you to have it managed."

"Well, I'm telling you I managed it, aren't I?"

"Which doubtless saved your life. I assume you're at the rectory?"

"I am. I was wondering whether I should contact Babylon."

"Go to the police? You should have done that last night."

"Frankly, it didn't seem to make much sense. What was I going to tell them? I never saw the man. I knew they'd find the car, and if they did it would probably have his fingerprints. That might be useful, but nothing much else, certainly not anything I could contribute."

"Those aren't reasons for neglecting to make a prompt report. Something like that happens, you go to the police."

"Jim, let's not kid ourselves. There's very little law in this place. There's good people and bad people, and so far the first outweigh the second. Even if the police were all angels, they have neither the equipment, nor the manpower, nor a government with sufficient political will to make law enforcement possible. They're already up over their heads with unsolved murders. They don't need some white type coming in to fuss over having a gun poked in his side. I'm alive. There's a whole lot of dead people out there and a whole lot of murderers on the loose."

"You sound like a lunatic on the loose. Look, you've no transportation there, have you?"

"Well, the fellow took the car."

"Okay. I'm going to get there as soon as I can. I should be able to leave here in a few minutes and the drive shouldn't take me more than an hour or so, though it is Friday afternoon and there may be a bit of traffic. I'll take you down to the station in Shining Waters."

"All right, if you think that's the thing to do."

"Look, Martin. Here's the thing. If a criminal needs a car for nefarious purposes, don't you think a twenty-five year-old VW Bug is a pretty odd choice? What concerns me is that the man may have been after you and not the car."

"Why on earth would anyone want to harm me?"

"Well, that's what we have to figure out."

"But he had me right there. He could have done whatever he wanted."

"That's true. Maybe he was acting on someone else's orders. Maybe he wasn't sure you were you. Or maybe he was after someone else that he mistook you for—me, for one. That's why we need to go to the police. So just stay there, out of trouble, till I arrive in *my* little blue VW Bug. Okay?"

"Okay, Father Jim. I'll be here."

He was waiting outside, enjoying the feel of the air after rain had washed it, of the mellow afternoon light that reminded him of autumn, of fruit ready to be picked. He was looking up into the roof of the shed. It was pretty sound. There was just one hole, which they could patch with tar, as Calvin had suggested, at least for the time being.

He was pleased with their efforts. He and Calvin had anchored the four uprights into solid blocks of concrete that went deep down. They had done a bit of work on the old floor of tamped-down marl; it was still a bit ragged but would do for now. And if they used some lattice on two parallel sides, it would make an open-ended meeting hall that could hold maybe twenty-thirty people. The youth could use it to hold meetings, and the Mothers' Union could use it, and the St Vincent de Paul Society that he hadn't yet organized properly.

Mère barked. Martin saw the youngster ricochet through the gate, as if someone had hurled him against something and he was bouncing back. One arm was holding his side, and blood was on his shirt. Calvin stumbled the short distance towards the shed, grabbed one of the corner supports and using it as a sort of launching pad, lunged towards him.

"Fada, go in..."

Martin heard the two shots, felt them coming before they hit. The boy fell first.

Church was full. Churchyard was full. The older folk among the crowd outside sat on chairs in the shed for the rain had drizzled on and off all day. The line of mourners climbed the hill, saw the two coffins on display, went back and fell in place along the route to the cemetery, which was further down the road, beside the ruins of the old church.

Trees and bush wailed in an un-seasonal high wind.

The archbishop, the superior and twenty other priests presided at the funeral service. Afterwards, at Lucky's insistence, the Waters youth took turns walking the coffins, side by side, down to the graveyard. Masses of local media came, newspaper people and radio and TV folks. Foreign media came too. His mother did not come.

The Mothers' Union took care of the food after the funeral. They fed everybody. The priests made sure there was liquor enough. As the coffins sank into the ground, there was a prolonged chorus of shots, perhaps a gun salute, from somewhere nearby in the bush.

Mère had seven puppies. Constantia took the strongest one, a handsome rusty beast with a fine feather of a tail. She wondered if they would have killed him in his right dress, with his priestly collar on.

"Once on the shores of
the stream, Senegambia..."

For Drew, Nalo, and my Great-Gran

I don't know how this thing I still calling 'my life' come so, for one time it had so many bright things. Even my dreams, long, clear as spring water, down to the colours of people's clothes, and pictures hanging on the wall, and what-you-can-see-through-the-window. Trew always say she don't know nobody dream so. And is true. I spin dreams like tapestry, so fine they return again and again, like they know they weave so well, woof and warp, that they deserve a person to look at them, touch them and feel them, over and over.

Take my Trew dream. In it, I see Trew at last, for the first time in how many years. How many years?

Don't recall when I first start dreaming that I see her again. One time, we meet finally in a fancy Paris restaurant. Another time is in a ritzy part of London. These places we meet up in is new to me, not any place I been, but I know is Paris and London all the same. Always I say to Trew how I glad it is real, the actual meeting, at last. And Trew is the same: rat face and pointy nose and small body bending forward a bit above the waist, little feet getting smaller towards the toes, as though they don't rightly belong on the ground and should maybe be touching on some other element, probably air.

Help. Something running in my body. Beating in it. Like maybe is a meeting house and the cacique talking with the tribe. Like maybe ten, twenty drums, thumping, thumping.

Is spring, and I come by bus from Miami to New York. Mrs Rita Whitter get acquainted with my Auntie Elsie because the Whitters give a chalice in memory of their son Alex, a twenty-year-old white youth that they beat to death in a Florida town because he try to break up a lynch mob. The chalice come by serendipity to my Uncle Roger's church in a bruck-down part of Kingstown. Auntie Elsie and Mrs Whitter stay fast friends long after the three hundred pounds of my uncle fall into heaven one Sunday morning when he vesting for Mass.

Because I going to visit America, Auntie Elsie give me Mrs Whitter phone number in Boston. When I call her she is not there but Matt who is now her one-son say he can drive me to Carole Ann wedding in Boston, for it just happen he going to be in New York that week and he going home to Boston the very Saturday morning. So said, so done. We drive four hours straight and reach the reception place and I jump out of Matt car and crash the wedding.

"Oh Clarabella!" Carole Ann say, "I can't believe you came all that way!"

And the groom kiss me, and all the white Irish women declare they glad to see me, the brown gyal. So they say, anyway, as they smilingly call me "brown gyal," half-bold and half-blushing, like we all gone back to the country day school. And I laugh, cause for sure I still poor as puss, but, as I consider them, I know I look like a million dollars. I look down at my mesh stockings and my brown sack dress and my chocolatey-gold shoes with heels you could spear a fish with. I see the deep brown of me, and the not-quite-so-brown of Trew, who is also there, with her slip of a self, looking mighty fine. I decide that she and I look muy preciosa. Not flashy. Just bright and polished. Mighty fine.

I remember how the reception place light up, as if, between Trew and me, we bring in the sun. As if we-self summon, beyond that great light, the blue, carrying-on-forever sky. As if, according to some invisible webbing, together we are part of a vast brown drum skin waiting for a promise to sound against it...

That is the last time I see Trew.

I need to sing. It focus my mind, make me feel better about these dreams and memories fading in and out, hard to hold onto and mix up into each other so I don't know which is which. Have to think hard to even dredge up the song. What I remember is only patches. Still, I going sing whatever come.

Once on the shores of the stream Senegambia
something and something gather to dance...

I could never tell you how bad I want to sing the whole song. How bad I dying to just open my mouth and sing it right out. I can't do that, though, no mind how hard I try. So I turn my hand make fashion. Cut frock to fit cloth. Sing my song out loud inside, the bits and pieces that come. You know the way. White people say one swallow don't make summer. That always make me laugh. Black people take one mosquito make summer. You just got to have the making inclination, is all.

Is not much I can see from here where I lying down. If is eyesight you trusting, the place don't seem to have neither top nor side, wall nor ceiling. Seem like is outside, but it feel close-in. It put me in mind of one of them inside-outside room that was a big fashion one time—which time, I not too sure. Inside this big-big outside-inside room is a giant sloping grassy field, with deep blue sky up so, and somewhere nearby, for you can hear the water lap-lapping and sometime it splash and the spray blow on you, somewhere nearby, a sea.

And it seem like we lying here in the sunlight—also don't know why I know is *we* for I can't see nobody, but I know is we—each one in a hammock maybe, or one of them big porch swings, long enough to lie down in, wide so you could sleep. And, just like I hear water, I smell the crisp salt smell of sea. And I see trees in the distance for my far vision is clear enough, but the things I think are near to me seem fuzzy, edges blotching, melting into one another.

I smell jasmine strong-strong when night fall, or more true, when the light fade...

A small woman. Skin very black. Hair very white. Fine, crinkly hair. Look like a head of white cotton candy. She eating a mango, laughing and serious one time. The last of the juice running down her chin and she still sucking hard on a nearly dry seed with some stringy blonde hairs hanging off it.

"So is me them send you to with that kind of question, Vinnie? Well, I know why. Is cause they know Gran going to answer you true-true, never mind you small. You see that weenie you have in front of you? Someday it going find a warm place to put itself, inside of some nice girl that going to love you with her whole heart. And it going be so excited and happy it not going to able to contain itself. It going stand up strong and dance around a while, and then it going to spill some sweet-sweet water. And that's going to make a baby. Your water in her belly going to make a pikni for you and she. Now what you think about that?"

The boy look down at his dark brown body. Put his

head oneside to consider. Then he say: "Granny, me going make plenty pikni like that." And he laugh and run off, head down considering the weenie that is going to do this splendid thing.

And the old sugar candy head woman say: "I hopes to God you live so long, my baby. Now they harvesting egg and seed. Now they raising human being like pig and chicken. Soon they going to tell we who to breed and who to barren. And I know who belly they going to lock down first."

She shake her head and slide the mango seed from her mouth. It is white now and only one-two blondish hairs straggle from it. She put it in a basket full of other seeds, dry same way, and walk off, balancing it, sure and steady, on her head. While she walking, she talking:

"Once upon a time, Brer Anansi was hungry bad, more hungry than he ever hungry before in his life, for a wicked famine was on the land. Brer Anansi hungry, him wife hungry, and the poor little spider-pikni them dying of starvation..."

That brown Trew girl, she got so much money the touch of the tar-brush don't hardly matter in the hoity-toity Country Day École du Sainte Marie Mère de Jésus, where I was the one so-so black scholarship pikni. Besides, is probably true that only we, with our Antillean eye that search out mixed blood at a glance, never mind how far back it go, only we would see that long ago some black warrior or some feisty mama did bless her family.

That girl save me. Make me laugh and sing and play in the rain. Make me don't too notice how them white gyal pikni look on me, how them run them finger over my skin like is accident, then gallop round the corner to pretend to blow away the blackness, or take eraser rub it out, or wash it off with a flourish in the goldfish pond.

Hear Trew: "You too foolish, Clarabella. In this school, only you and I look like we do. You've never heard of scarcity value? That's what we have, *querida*. Like diamonds. We are exploding prisms of light. *Muy preciosa*."

I smile, a lopsided monkey-face smile.

Trew say: "*Dice: 'Soy preciosa'. Dice: 'Somos preciosas'.*"

Was the first Spanish I learn.

Here I say it now, every minute, over and over, like a chant. "*Soy preciosa. Somos preciosas.*'"

I got to smile when I think of me and this singing-singing! When they make me sing at the country day school, I spit out the song. Now I only too ready to open my mouth and keep singing, if by God's love I could hold onto a melody and remember the words good enough.

Baby mother have a something,
Baby mother something have a something,
His locks is like something another ...

Is only some skemps bits of song and story come, but I glad for anything at all, same like only scrapses of my life float up. I don't think bout it too much, for it frighten me bad. Is like somebody capture me one day, and drag me away from home and friends and family, and places I know and love; like they take for themselves my memory of times and weather, the things I say and promises I make. Sometime I not even certain if how I speak is mine.

I am studying but I am working too, in a big city where it is cold sometimes, so cold that snow fall down out of the heavens when it ready. I am not a person from a snowing place, though. I know this because every time I step outside my body squeeze in on itself, away from the hacking wind, away from the miserable freezing weather.

I am hurrying on my way to meet some people for I see this ad in the paper and I phone the number and they tell me to come.

WANTED: Women of colour between the ages of 18 and 35 to participate in a long-term health study. Must be willing to submit to a prescribed diet and exercise regimen. No drugs, vitamins, or supplements. Payment for participation.

I will get $50.00 a month if they accept me. I need the extra dollars.

When I get to the address, I find that is a medical

place, like a small hospital, all white and clean and smelling like fresh air. I reach on time and at the information desk they show me where to go. I tell myself to be glad that I get this opportunity, to believe that sometimes a person get a break.

The lady that I see when I knock on Room 66 is businesslike. She give me a form to fill out. She say as she hand it to me, "I hope it's not too long nor too intrusive."

I give her back the full-up form and ask if is only me that come.

"Oh no! We've seen everyone else for the day," she say. "Yours was the last appointment."

She send me into a room to take off all my clothes and put on a gown with blue flowers on it and lie down and wait for the doctor. The room is a cool blue and there is Christmas carols playing softly and I drop asleep.

This place make me nervous from the beginning, for somewhere in the very pit of my stomach, I know it really don't go so, never mind what I think I seeing, what I imagine I smelling and touching. Somebody someplace some long time ago tell me to trust that funny feeling you get in your belly-bottom, and my belly-bottom say this not no large space. If it so big, why I feel like I got a weight top of me, like things pressing me in from two sides? Why I feel like I in a small tunnel, and it getting smaller, the top getting closer to my belly every day?

Every so often, I wake up and find I not rocking in the hammock or swing or whatever it be, anymore. I still lying flat, but I in water, clear, pretty, blue water, with what look like white sand under me, never mind I can't touch bottom. I think maybe this is exercise time, and, tell the truth, it come easy to float or swim or just splash around, for it is cool and wet. Clever as they be, they would have to come good to make me think I swimming in water if is not so. I don't know bout the white sand, but I pretty sure the water is water.

Is always warm and sunny when we swimming, though we don't actually see no sun. This is the one time I feel like somebody again, like a ordinary person in a usual place doing a ordinary thing. I know that I must come from a place with sun and sea because I take to the salty water and the wash of the waves like a fish, and because this is the one time I feel like I am real, with at least a familiar now and maybe a time to look forward to.

Help! Somebody, help! Feet running in my body again. Beating time in it. A sweet rhythm but I fraid, for it just drumming on, all by itself, and I don't know what cause it. For sure, it going bring something. Is a noise with a promise.

Mark you, that Trew girl try my patience when she ready. Like when spring come and she find her way onto the next-door college campus, way down by the Quonset hut where none of we suppose to go, and she discover some bird that drop out a tree and bruck him foot, or some mangy squirrel that losing it fur, and bring it back into the day school, up into my room.

"You keep him, Clarabella," she say. "You know they're afraid of you. Nobody's going to come in here, into this room, to look for anything. It just needs to stay a day or two, till the bones knit." All this time, she taking a couple matchstick and some string and making splint for the bird foot.

I roll my eyes. I say, "I don't want no bird in my room. Is your bird. You find him. You keep him."

"Is not a him, is a her," Trew say. How she could know, I always wonder. "You don't have any feeling for a wounded member of your own sex?"

"I got plenty feeling for me, myself, and I," I tell her. "Them three wounded members of my own sex, they takes up all my energy. And doing the work, homework and housework and work-at-the-switchboard work, that I need to do to stay in this place and keep my head up amongst the five hundred likes of you. You think it easy?"

She laugh. "Not the likes of me, for sure," she say. "There ain't no likes of me here, except of course for you."

She put the bird down in the cover of my straw sewing basket.

"I don't business with you, rich girl. You okay, I suppose, but I can't afford to business with you. What I have to do is to survive in this place, and I not going able to do that if I providing lodging for your birdies and your squirrels and all the other half-dead things you drag in here from out the bush!"

I give them lodging anyway. I figure what go round come round. Maybe I get back some loving care when I need it.

...drumming again, the beat a little faster, like feet trotting. I not sure why I so fraid for it. Maybe because it is in my body and I don't know how it come to be there...

One time when I was swimming I see something. It happen quick-quick, ten, fifteen seconds or so, but I damn sure that I see what I see. I on my back in the sea one day, and suddenly, as if everything blink like a gigantic eyelid, there is no sky no more, no sun and grassy slope and trees. Instead, I am squinting against a blinding light. And I discern that I am under a very high dome of plastic or glass or maybe even ice. In a flash, but clear as day, I see the round icy shell a far way up, and I see that against the sides are wide shelves that extend above one another into the dome space, big enough to hold a body though they all empty just now. And I see layers and layers of thin, shining threads like very fine wire, worked all the way up the sides of this gigantic upside-down bowl. And the last thing I see, or almost see, is bodies, hundreds of dark bodies like mine, each packaged in a cylinder like a slab of chocolate in its own wrapping, and all washing back and forth like me in this huge container of water.

I blink, and when I open my eyes good and wide, I see myself all alone in the sea, the light of the almost-sun bright around me, the waves lap-lapping in my ears, the salt smell filling up my nostrils till it burning my lungs, and the never-ending blue-blue sky over my head.

As I trying to figure all this out, I see the outside-inside room flicker again for a split second, and I see the pool again with all the bodies in it, only dark bodies, and I see some pale-pale people in white uniform pulling a young woman, naked as the day she born, from the pool. Her belly is huge, like she been drinking the pool water and it swell her up. And she is screaming and screaming, like she stark raving mad. Then it vanish in a flash, and a blast of jasmine scent overpower my nose.

I know something is missing. Or maybe I am missing something. So many scraps. The scraps of songs and stories I am trying so hard to remember. Where I come from... Where this place is... How I reach here... How I reach from Kingstown to the country day school... What happen to Trew...

I long for a deep abiding sleep. I long to get rid of the heavy thing that pressing down on me, pushing in on me from two sides, never mind the distant blue-blue sky, and the soothing lap of the waves, and the sweet smells of flowers.

Now, in this place, sleep is not by choice; it come by its own bidding once the dimness start to creep over. By the time the real darkness set in, we knock out like we dead. If you ask me, it must come through a tube or a wire, though I can't see neither one nor the other coming into me, like food must come, for I can't recall eating no food from I find myself here. And we, for I know is we, we rise same way, as the light come, like morning glory and buttercup. Something poke us, promising that if we open our eyes, some good thing going happen to make it worth the effort.

Nothing good like that up to now, though. Not up to now.

"...and quick as a flash, Brer Anansi drop the brick onto Brer Snake back, and then he look at Brer Rabbit and say, "Next time Brer Rabbit, don't trouble trouble till trouble trouble you..."

I don't see the old black lady telling the story, but I know is her voice, and I think it remind me of how somebody else talk. Maybe my Auntie Elsie.

When I do get to see her, she is lying down, hands at her side, feet bare. Still, so still, like a dead somebody, except that when I look close, her small chest is rising and falling like she in deep sleep. Her face is lit, like the black skin is giving off a deep blue light, and the countenance, and her whole self it seem, resting, every muscle in repose. Strange, though, at the very same time, every cell lock onto something.

On the floor beside her I see some things. Her head-tie, for the cotton candy hair is loose and having its own way, like a wisp of white cloud caught on the top of her black head. Her spectacles and her apron. A old leather belt. Her thick pink old-woman stockings. Some shiny things too: a narrow gold ring; a pair of silver bangles.

When I look again I catch my breath. I notice she is not lying on anything: she is floating. Floating maybe a hand's breadth off the ground. I stare at this impossible thing and see her very slowly rise, still deep in sleep, still glowing, still resting, still whole-self holding onto some great thing... And I look close in her face and it strike me that her broad flat nose and her high cheekbones remind me of Mama.

I think one time when I wake, something misfire, for I find I feeling different. Not good. Not comfortable. I draw breath quick and realize that one of the things my body forget is bad feelings. Is only the drumming that come near bad feeling, and, where the drumming concerned, is not my body that is in distress but something else, deep inside.

And I give thanks for how my belly feel, sick, like

everything in it going to come up through my throat and pour over me. And as I gather this discomfort to me, I sort of see a shape that I recall but cannot name, a shape like a walking river, like a road hurrying on. I see it only faint, for a brief while, but I know it as my road, my river, and I think, "Something is taking my self from me. Maybe all these good feelings is why I can't find the thread, the story of me, the thing that make me myself."

I make up my mind right that minute to encourage bad feelings, for maybe they help me remember myself. I think to myself that somewhere in my body, in my skin and blood and bone, is the writing of my life. I think if I can get it back, I can figure out this whole thing: what is real and what is not. Why I am here, and how I come to be here. And who is doing all of this. And why.

Strange how life go, contrary like. I want to rest, to sleep, and same time I desperate to make myself feel bad, so I can get back the thread of my life.

Once on the shores of the stream Senegambia
something and something gathered to dance
and something and brazen and something for picking...

Is 'mangoes'! 'Mangoes for picking!' I wrap the one word, like a enormous blanket, around myself.

I smile a big smile as I think of days at school with Trew. How she always taking care of things. Specially small things. How she say I am precious; we are precious. How she say me and she is "like". I don't at this minute have in my head anyone but Trew that I am "like". The dark bodies in the pool, if they really there, then I guess me and them is like. But I not sure. My belly-bottom say like on the outside don't necessarily mean like on the inside. I need people who is like to me on the inside.

I think it's the memory of Trew that start me singing and telling story and telling about the scraps that I remember. I think is the hurt of the white girls making fun of me at the country day school that make me wonder if pain, bad feelings, will help to bring things back to my mind.

I count up what I have. I think my head still working pretty good. And I know I can trust my belly-bottom, for is it make me smell out something funny in the first place. And I have the scraps: the pieces of song and story, and the snips of my life that are so clear, is like I still there living through their brief moments. They have stuff in them, inklings that I must try to put together.

A short black man, with almost no hair, who give me a silver three-penny piece when I get good marks at school...

A old house with high ceilings and a deep cellar underneath and a bush beside that bloom white flowers before rain come...

Manatee, a great big sad mama manatee, lying still on

the black sand beach, beside a string of blue and red canoes turn upside down and weary with peeling paint. The canoes have names like "Saga Bwoy" and "Saints Marching In" and "Penny Reel" ...

A graveyard with a gate that have a rusty lock that nobody don't ever open, and graves that don't have no headstone, and a high brick wall...

Barge, barge that grow on the barge tree, the fruit like short see-though green tubes, bearing straight from the dark tree stem, so sour that Mama always say, "sour like barge..."

Mama, slim and smiling, who is the exact stamp of Auntie Elsie, down to the scar above her top lip and the mole on her neck. How that could be?

And the dreams, the Trew dreams...

When is this and where is this and why the pieces slip away each time I look to grab them with my fist of memory?

They more real for sure than this place that's all round me, here and not here, with sun we can't see, and sea that's not sea, and odours that kick you like strong drugs when them ready.

And it come to me for the first time that I been seeing a old black lady, a woman with fine white crinkly hair on her head, thin, with strength tie up into her like a piece of rope and a voice and face that remind me of my Auntie Elsie. And one time I see her talking to a little boy, naked as the day he born...

And the dome house, and all the rest that I know is here, never mind I can't see them, and the bodies swimming in the pool, and the pale people in white coat, and the screaming, big belly woman...

The noise again, the feet galloping now, and still there is nothing, not a thing I can do to stop it. Drums beating, beating, like the pulsing of blood, and feet, running, running, like is to save their very life.

The running so insistent, so harnessing my body that it leave me no choice. For the first time, I give it no resistance. I let myself go with it, like a tiny boat in a strong current, this noise like a whole bunch of people tumbling towards something, galloping, galloping, and still keeping time. A herd of people-elephants lunging through my belly.

Craziness. How I could have a bunch of people in me? People can't have people in them—only if they crazy, and in all of this it don't occur to me once that is mad I mad. Except they making baby of course, and nobody make twenty and thirty baby at a time.

And besides, if I make a guess and try put two and two together (for my brain crank up now), the cotton candy head lady did say that is black people body they going lock down when they start deciding who to breed and who not to. So chances are, if is somebody lock me up in here, lock up a whole lot of black women in here, is to make sure them don't breed. I think of the screaming woman with the swell-up belly and my own belly that seem like it getting bigger. Maybe they feeding us something in the swimming water, something to make us swell up and burst, mash up our womb...

And it come to me that I don't even know who I fighting with. For certain, is not the people dress up in white uniform, for I know them is just orders-takers, people following instructions. Black people can tell that kind. Easy.

Black people take one mosquito make a summer... Black people have a making spirit... Black people can tell orders-takers... Black people is forever singing, dancing...

It is the old black lady who look like Auntie Elsie and her two arms full, for she is holding two big baskets, and, when I look inside, they are full of small white bundles, like the way, on ironing day, we first sprinkle the white clothes, after they done being washed and bleached in the sun, and we blue them and dry them, and then wrap them in on themselves and set them to wait their turn for ironing.

I am thinking, "Poor lady, so much to iron" when I see at the top of each bundle, a pale small head with stringy blonde hairs hanging from it, and wide open, blue-blue eyes.

I think they capture my brain. I don't want to be in this place. I never take up myself and come here. They holding me against my will, chain or no chain.

I don't even finish thinking this good before I feel a buzz pass through my body. Run deep into it, and right straight through it. A sweet feel-good ripple that thrill me way inside.

"They reading my head," I say to myself. "They must know I up to something. But how they could know?"

Same time I feel a wetness on my forehead, a bead of water. And I remember sweat.

"Perspiration," I think. "They see me sweating."

And I know for certain that all around me, above, at the sides, and below, whatever I feel bearing down and pressing in is a thing that is also watching me. A thing that not only watch, but tell somebody what it see. And this watching somebody arrange to do things to my body. To reach way inside it, to make it feel good, and so, for sure, make it feel bad, if they want.

I don't know what I can do about that.

Something is leaking slow, slow, into my head, pushing, like a word on the tip of my tongue that I know I going to speak eventually, but it taking its time to let me call it.

Then I realize. I can't move, not foot or hand or trunk of my body. Fingers and toes and the muscles on my face, ears, nose, those I could move, and the ones I use to pee, but is like somebody tie down the big parts of me.

I is one big jackass! How I never see that before? We only can move hand and foot and body when we swimming...

But there must be something I can do, some way to

say that this is my body that I have charge of, with a life and story of its own. I think of pee. Maybe I can pee... And that very minute I feel wetness under me, creeping out from my groin in a big warm patch. Littlemost I smile, but I remember the eyes-all-around and I let my face be. Glory hallellujah! I pee up myself. I. My pee. *I wet up myself with my pee like a baby*. I bask in this glorious feeling for a while, but I am careful to hold my face still, so no smile nor sweat will betray me.

But now there is a big problem: how to do things without they know. I can only take action on the inside, since outside I cannot lift a finger. I make a virtue of necessity. I fix my face. I speak to my skin, the small muscles in my neck, my jaw, my teeth, the hair on my head. I tell them to be absolutely quiet, so all this going on inside me will belong only to me.

I decide to rest my brain, empty it out, give it a break, for it don't gallop like this since I come here. I don't hear the drums this long time. When I think about it, it come to me that they now going non-stop, but, since everything else going so fast, the drumming noise is just part of one big enormous galloping, rushing, thundering ruckus...

... pulse pumping, drums beating, feet running, running, like is for their very life...

And the old black lady, floating, floating in the air, just come into my mind, same so. And I think, I going to try to be as cool and resting and relaxed as she. And I sure again that her head was deep into something. And not just her head, but her old black body. So it seem I need to be deep into something same time as I resting quiet.

Which is well enough, but deep into what? Still and all, I going to try, try to reach to the place where she reach. I going to empty my head right out, and I going to beg whatever is out there that... That what? Well, whatever is out there that is decent, and mean no harm, to let me fix my whole self onto it. Is the best I can do. Can't think of nothing better.

As I struggle to drop things out of my head, and is a terrible struggle, for suddenly so much things that I don't understand is happening, so much scraps of things that I remember crowding into my brain, I hear a soft chanting sound coming from far-far. I think it say something like "mah rah nah tah" and, though it is tuneless, only a drone, I have this sense that I am following it, hearkening to it and it alone, and traveling with it, up and up. My body change gear, as it lift, and things fall away from it, from me.

Somewhere in the warm red blackness behind my closed eyes, I see a point of pulsing blue light, a blue that is not green blue, or yellow blue or red blue, but the true-true blue of maybe the light inside a candle flame, maybe the light of the life inside of things.

Then I am lost in whatever it is that is there.

After, long after, I sleep, and in that sleep I get a terrible vision, a vision concerning Trew. She lying on a gurney, flat like I lying now, her face death-green. The place tile with shiny blue porcelain tiles that put me in mind of the birthing room in a hospital, though how I know what that look like, I can't tell. It have some people in gowns standing over her, and I know they are doctoring people for they hold shiny instruments. I spot one as the head, for growing from his forehead is a bulb of white light, and he is holding a sword of light: sometimes long, sometimes short; sometimes bright orange, sometimes pale yellow so I can barely see it. He use the sword-light to cut Trew body, then he get busy like a ferret. I see him pulling small bloody parcels out of her, delivering them to a endless line of hands that receive them as he pass them over his shoulder.

"Oh heavens!" I think to myself. "She sick. She sick unto dying. They cutting, cutting away the sickness, and they can't finish because there is so much of it."

I so frighten that I check to see if is really Trew. I look hard in her face and I know is she, yes.

"A fine breeder," I hear the man with the light sword say.

Then I run my eyes down her body, and come to her middle. Her belly is a huge bloody shell with fifteen, maybe twenty navel strings hanging from the sides, draining into the womb-space. When I look in her face again, she is weeping, weeping, her eyes moving crazy from left to right, then to left again, hunting, hunting for something...

I stumble into wakefulness, like the sight make me buck my toe and so I wake up.

Again, there is a blinding light in my eye. I can clearly see the dome, the glass shelves extending out into the dome space, the warren of wires. I am rising, rising, like I am on a see-through elevator. I know that they have chained me, hand and foot and torso, to a gurney. I see four, maybe five, pale people in white uniforms beside me. I cannot see the ones at my feet for my belly is so big that I cannot see beyond it.

Then a tide of good-feelings washes over me, and my insides quiver, and I am in my hammock again, the sun warm, the sea murmuring, the salt smell biting my tongue.

It startle me, I tell no lie, when I see Trew running to meet the old cotton candy lady, and, following behind her like a line of ducklings, more little blonde children, with heads trailing wisps of blonde hair, and eyes blue as the blue-blue far-away sky in this impossible place. As usual, it is bright, clear, just as if I am there. And I move to the old lady and speak, and this language I know is mine.

"Whose pikni?" I say. "Why so much of them? And why them looking so?" But she don't hear me. Trew don't hear me. Them just going on together about their business.

I watching as the old lady and the children follow Trew to a grassy place with a big round flat-topped stone in the middle. I watch the old lady take out from deep in her thick layers of skirt, for she look like she wearing clothes on top of clothes, a long shiny thing like a saw. And Trew take out two things from her skirts that look like sticks with something big and round at the top.

"Lawd, no!" I make to shout. "They is only children. You can't kill them!"

The duckling children form a circle inside a bigger circle. From her skirts, again, the black lady produce a thin bit of metal and she take it and start to scratch at the saw. The children in the small circle stamping their feet. The children in the big circle clapping their hands. And Trew shaking the sticks and the old lady singing:

Once on the shores of the stream, Senegambia
parrots and peacocks gathered to dance.
Trees with oranges brazen and mangoes for picking
lower their branches, sway to the music...

And I laugh out loud, for I know now they are gourds, and that this is a dance to the music of saw and maracas, and the blonde nigger children—the ducklings, the laundry—blue eyes and all, they are all Trew's brown babies. And they are not lost, not lost.

I look at my belly. I see it is higher today than ever

before. I study the tight shiny black mound. To date, it don't jump. When it jump, I know I am in trouble and I am done with trouble at one time. I smile.

They think they making one set of people, but I here making sure is another.

I work and work to teach the children in my belly. I tell them every single thing that has happened to me that I remember. I sing them every song. I recite them my dreams. I show them their ancestors. I relate, again and again, every story, all the bits and pieces that I know. I swear by the bits of my life, that I will reclaim them, keep them, for I have told them they are precious, and marked them with my words and songs, our words and songs, stories and dreams. I think of Trew and ratchet up my will one notch. After her, how many of us before they reach me?

It is a drum. The pulse of a drum. It is the noise of my body. Our bodies. The driving of all of our hearts.

So I lying here, gazing at my tight belly. I sure I see one tiny ripple and I catch my breath. Is time. I am in their birthing room and they going cut me now. And the drumming galloping noise I been hearing in my head will finally go. And maybe I will go with it. Yellow hair, yes, and blue-blue eyes, but they going to be my babies, black babies, the mould of our story growing on their bones.

Light fade. Time to sleep now. I going sleep easy. Going dream the children drumming, dancing, singing a Senegambian song.